We of Death
and Taxes

We of Death and Taxes

TERRY MIDKIFF

iUniverse, Inc.
Bloomington

We of Death and Taxes

iUniverse books may be ordered through booksellers or by contacting:

iUniverse
1663 Liberty Drive
Bloomington, IN 47403
www.iuniverse.com
1-800-Authors (1-800-288-4677)

ISBN: 978-1-4620-4539-6 (sc)
ISBN: 978-1-4620-4544-0 (hc)
ISBN: 978-1-4620-4540-2 (ebk)

Library of Congress Control Number: 2011915129

Cover design, Terry Midkiff

Printed in the United States of America
iUniverse rev. date: 10/12/2011

In this world, nothing can be said to be certain except death and taxes.

—Benjamin Franklin

Prologue

Greetings. I'm sitting here . . . some light years, it seems, from where I was sitting the last time. How do I begin? Let me tell you, through no shortage of luck and iron have I made it to our present age. Here I sit. Hunched over my little control pad. Checking in on what's going on. And just what the hell is going on!

I walk over, put on some coffee. Walk back to my chair.

It could get ugly again. It's always been this way. Ever since I can remember.

I watch my controls. Seems this is going to take a long time. Naturally. The id has dug in, but the superego never stops. Ah well. Here we go . . .

PART 1

1

As I journey through this absurdity called existence, I am struck most by the lack of an endgame.

I feel as if I've spent so long seeing and experiencing things, so long spent fighting, so long spent counter attacking and rebuilding that I can't do anything else but fight to keep on fighting and one day hold it off long enough to escape. (Into what? I only wish for an extended vacation.)

It is now the end of August. Not that that means anything, just wanted to get that clear before I started.

I've decided I'm not moving anywhere. Binghamton was a joke. I'll either move back to Niwot or down to Denver. With my little trollop, that is. Charlotte. Yes. I am living with a young woman now.

But I have suitable employment. Yes. Tomorrow I plan to attend a meeting at work regarding an increase in our monthly rate for health insurance. I get to take in this small-time theater among the mid-classes of the early twenty-first-century throng that somehow spilt out into existence.

Yes. I adjust my little screen pad. I am in between visits. Visits to the outside world. Some of them take a very long time.

Yes. Everyone suffers from addiction. Information overload. It's hilarious what we've come to. Everyone's a strung-out neurotic.

Life couldn't be more absurd at this point. Everything is perpetually ripe. It's just one big harvest. Notice how everything still keeps happening. It's fascinating.

Mm. But as my girlfriend and I prepare to look for an apartment, my mind has become increasingly active. Restless. Tortured. As I contemplate the absurdity of so many situations in the world, I've decided that murder is what's done to life, not humans. Even so, it fairly intoxicates me on some level. And for the life of me, I still can't decide which is better, God or business. Ah. God. Business. But what an interesting time in the life of homo sapiens. Youth! Blessed youth! Ah youth! Time of folly and blooming strength! Why, I feel like dancing even now! To the ballroom! And load my revolver!

*   *   *

I'm all moved in. I'm in a new apartment now. I've been recuperating. My girlfriend is at work.

I have to capture time like this to put into order the streaming flood of input and residue that collects. I live in what used to be called a nice neighborhood here in the Republic of Boulder, until it was gradually eroded by students and loudness and general lack of style.

My life is a scratch at an itch. Here and there, continuation. More days and years.

Yes. Everything has become a business. Entertainment. Life. Even meaning. But, how clever. After all, who doesn't like sugar! Who doesn't like the glistening, white pure-cane prostitution that lies at the heart of everything? Yes. What is America, if not Nature? And what is Nature?

(Mm. But what could be better? I snicker.)

Yes. The mass element of society lives together in relative comfort and ease ... fed on sugar, living in hives of info-drugged narcosis, tech-god entertainment and political-religious claptrap which serve to inhibit not only the ability to discern reality, but most innovative thought for the mass of the population.

(Mm. But what could be better? I snicker.)

In a few hundred years, it'll all be old again. The basis for something else to slowly grow out of it and then take it over. Just like it took over. And what of the severity of the change, the melting of truth into orange, smoky lava?

We're just one more ingredient in the volcano.
The bringer of death. The bringer of life. Something like the sun.

2

I look out my window. Outside there is activity, cars, lectures on chakras, hiking, the soul.

Charlotte and I had dinner last night on Pearl Street. On the outdoor mall. At Cheesecake Factory. Yes.

We sat outside munching away on apple pastries or some such. Pedestrians ambled up and down. Artsies. Natives. Tourists.

Yes. It's all here in Boulder. Age of Aquarius. Porpoises. Whales. Pathways of the soul. Bermuda Triangle. Atlantis. Possible aliens. Visits. Promises to come back. A bazaar of the soul with all manner of spiritual goodies and rainbows. Mental conditions. Needs and wants. Childhood.

Yes. It's all here. Mountain bikes, rock climbing, tree climbing. On any afternoon, the hills are awash with the sound of sweat. With testosterone. Estrogen. Yes. Everyone is in outdoor hyperdrive. It's always the Olympics. They never end. It's always the next event, the next match, the next competition. Downhill Slalom Ass-Spanking. Cross Country Alpine Shaving Cream! World class competition!

Yes. But everything is kept in order by . . . the Bike Path Nazis. Yes. The Bike Path Nazis pass you in great numbers. With their helmets. Their protein pills. Their carbohydrate packs and their little black pants. Zoom! A whole pack of them flies by. Six or eight or ten. Locked in unison. Angling around the curve with their legs. Their racing programs.

Off they go. Into the blue. The horizon stretches out, takes them in . . .

The Republic.

3

Shades of a New Epoch, Volume 1.

Relativity. Motion. The sight of atoms. All impossible as the sun. Days on end. Mood swings of weeks. I open my eyes. Walk down the hall at work. Turn over in my sleep. Drive home. Eternity.

I smoke, hack, cough into my screen. Every day I read of tragedy, various ridiculousness. The world is a tremendous source of entertainment. It's on every day. The news is now the news. News is the response to news. News is the response to everything. There'll be more tomorrow.

The next day . . .

Sex is ageless. A broken record below the belt. Time and again a skirt. Wagging along. The curve of summer. More inviting than God. Bent over for freedom.

Mm. I need to put away the smoke. Ahem. I wrap my robe. Light a cigarette.

My mind continually speeds up. Yes. I write passing fragments of Earth and hell unearth old spirits, record new fuels. Onward! Upward!

Right now, I am drilling sideways, attempting to break into the inner corridor. I left my watch there.

Yes, the current sociopolitical situation makes perfect sense to me. A comedy for the ages. Ah . . . layers of beauty blanket the land. I wonder and swell with it. Modern life. The beauty of death. Millions of faces screaming away at nothing.

Taking their turn. Ugly faces, mostly. Artless, unhappy faces. They want it! They get it!

I've never seen a more perfect set of circumstances. The power. Oh, the power to carve what you're given. To scour the landscape. Accept it as you would the highest honor. You think it's different. It's all the same.

Time and again, the end. The beginning. Convenient souls. Ones and O's.

Hilarious. The stomping elephant march of discontent that mankind is on. The greedy search for happiness. To meditate on it is to realize that it can only be explored within the general framework of a mental condition. A manhunt for fulfillment through the secrets of the earth.

A thousand years from now, it'll just be something else.

In the evenings, I sit and watch the lights of the city flicker off and on. The ethereal electric glow rising over the plains. I-36 corridor running north through the fields like a great Danube of hell. Hieronymus Bosch. Pieter Breugel. Plato's nephews.

Let it begin.

4

Shades of a New Epoch, Volume 2.

I'm sitting here smoking a cigarette at 1:00 a.m. The cat keeps running in and out of the room, disturbing my gentle Zen.

The night has come, crawling up over the mountains.

The upcoming weeks should prove fruitful. At present, my days move along in familiar disarray. I hear noises. Noises! Augh! I'm always hearing noises that I do not want to hear. Everyone around me is an idiot. Bill the landlord sits this afternoon trying to explain the difference in alternate current and direct current to me as he's installing a new electrical outlet. I nod up and down.

"Yeah yeah, just fix it."

Now I can finally say piss on everything. Heaven? Hell? Stop signs in your mind.

You live in the world. All the great spasmodic tentacled mess of it. All the banalities, the absurdity of it all, the strange, slow beauty to a day. All the earth edging and jerking along toward itself. The age demands what all ages demand: Acceptance! Continuation!

But we here are not concerned with such obviousness. What we are concerned with are localized, possible worlds. The worlds of our making.

And if I make it into my own little castle some day, it will be one of the true miracles of the age. I will sit back and idly smoke away the evenings with Charlotte and her breasts (my only true delight). I will celebrate the failure of it all. The victory of it all!

I scratch at an itch. Life bleeds away inside. The wheels turn and the chain clinks. Out the window, I can see a meadow. Green-breasted. Fertile. Like a new day. I drift off. I pass through bars and out into sunlight. I float through the afternoons. Through days. Weeks. Dimensions. Levels of self. Real history. Real future.

On it goes. Forming in the night like some strange fungus.

5

Here I am. Back from the dead.

How does it continue? Simple. How does a ball roll down a hill?

My spirit waxes. I'm floating through la-la land. My spirit wanes. I'm ready for bed.

Life comes down to hacking through chaos until your own path becomes clear.

All the weeks battled. The sum total of nothing. All the mind-numbed day-tangents. All the weekends. All the work weeks. The plans. The decisions. The new variables.

I sit here wiping the gunk of the day off my spirit.

I live at 327 Front Street now. I've moved yet again. A little shack. I don't speak any more. I snort. I snort and sit back and polish my hooves.

My girlfriend has gone somewhere. I'm living here now, where everyone is simple and everything is easy, in Louisville. Mainly because the rent is cheap and I could afford to move into this little rundown hut with a front yard and a little gate and trees and a shed in back.

I'm sitting here in my back bedroom now. Giggling at my hour of free time. But it's the rest of my life. I couldn't be happier.

God, where to begin?

I feel the urge to walk in to the kitchen now and pour a glass of wine.

Now then. Now that we've made it into the first decade of the twenty-first century. God, it's all been so ridiculous. I sit out here with my shack-job. Out here in the New West. I snicker at my little fence. I plod around in the yard, inspecting irregularities.

The thought of everything makes me want to take a nap. God . . . my life . . . moving forward into something like it is. It seems something like a trick or a dream, but I know it is no dream. It's only a dream spiritually. The things you think you need are not there. But do you know what you really need?

I climb back up into the moment. Fumble around for controls.

I've been up here from Austin five and a half years now. My friend Morton got me a job up here. And Bern. I work in an office. It's the longest time I've worked anywhere. It seems to be stretching out to infinity. Week after week, season after season, year after year.

But oh, the joy to sit here. Oh, the joy to sit here as the sun burns another day.

I consider the lines on my hands, light a cigarette.

We are trapped inside life. Trapped inside the dream. But you're free to define life, and to add your angle to the sculpture of it. Of civilization. Of history. Of mankind. The miracle. The mystery. The why. The because. Where anything is still possible. Whatever you can think up. Where health is. Where health grows. Where health exults in health.

Mankind is Lazarus, rising up into forever.
Mankind is a carbon smear on the blueprint of possibility.

6

Charlotte is out of town. I'm sitting here trying to think of a way to cool down the house more quickly. The cat is pacing back and forth, in and out of the bedroom.

Life travels with you, without you. It never lets up. I'm sitting here as the night burns away. My mind is a firefly on a summer evening. On the Serengeti. Midnight shift.

Life collides, breaks apart. Days fly back and forth. Into one another. Pieces of circumstance. Gravity. Endurance. A swirling of days and sensations. Weeks pass. Months. Life forms yet again, speeds up, begins to rotate. You see it for what it is, a clear, whirring eternity.

PART 2

1

November 30, 20___. Vermont.

I convinced my superiors to let me work from home.

I've moved again. I'm on the run now. Nothing ever works out. Animals die. People get to be too much.

I'm sitting here in bed now listening to Richard Wagner. A few weeks have passed. I do my work on a home computer now.

I live in the village of Vergennes, Vermont.

We rented the top floor of a large, green, two-story house in town. We picked this house out of a hat. I have no idea how it happened.

I walk around back in my room. I must see someone about my heart pains. *Eine kleine Nachtmusik.*

I'm sitting up here with *Jane Eyre*. On the island of Elba. I'm on the run again.

It snowed two feet yesterday. If I can make it through winter, I think everything will be okay. No matter. I've managed to escape once more.

I look out the window at the streetlight. At the village. At the snow. I look back in. A car drives by slowly. I light a cigarette. I've been trying to quit but I can't completely. There is nothing to equal the pleasure of smoking a cigarette, sitting in some big chair, and looking outside as the smoke curls up a lampshade.

The year is almost down the toilet. I hated it. Never have I worked harder to maintain sanity, finances, and health.

No matter. Assuming I don't have cancer or some sort of heart condition when I visit the doctor next month, I'm going to get high and chain-smoke for five hours.

2

Religion. In the end, everything is religion.

For there are as many worlds as there are kinds of pain. And pleasure, too. Onward!

3

Ah, we.

We have an uncertain past, an uncertain future. We exist in dreams, memories, transformations. We are at home in this place. We know nothing else. There is nothing else to know.

We are Icarus. We are Job. We are Lucifer.
We are at home.

4

Alone in my bedroom now. It's minus 4 degrees Fahrenheit outside. It has hit me, what I've done. The heater wheezes and moans. I look off, sneeze.

People? I write for seahorses . . . rocks . . . the king of the emeralds.

Alabaster, albino. All serious as a shoe.

5

How did the Abenaki make it through winter here? They didn't go out much, evidently. And the life expectancy was probably about nineteen.

My throat. Augh! I can't breathe properly. Just last week I had to go on supplemental oxygen. What a frozen, ridiculous state this is.

I look around, and consider my bed that I'm laying on now. My room. It's approximately nine by eleven feet. Books and magazines stacked into shelves. A few hundred or so. A print on the wall. A little table with Japanese lamp to my left. And the window and the closet straight up ahead. The door in the northwest corner closed. A womb. A nucleus.

Ordinarily I would be at my desk, but it is currently being used for other, more pedestrian purposes: making a living! Yes!

Move to Vermont. Move to Texas, Colorado, Mars! What's the difference?

But good news: my haircut went off without a hitch. A complete success! Success? What mental condition do I have? Do I have a condition? Well, marvelous then. More of it!

My condition is . . . it is no matter. Solitude. The cure: *Onward*. My medicine.

6

Monday evening. First day of the new work week! All I try to do now is waste time. Yes, waste time. Ha! Time is meant to be wasted. It's not precious. It's a bore beyond all imagining. Ahahhahhaaa, there. No, seriously. What I do with my days is a work of art, a sculpture. Ask not for whom the bell tolls, it tolls for me. Ahahaaa. Oh shit. What is happening to me? Ahem. Maybe I should smoke a cigarette.

I just bought a fresh pack! No, no I can't.

Oh shit, where was I? Ah yes, time. Yes, yes, I waste time. That is my main preoccupation. No, my main occupation these days.

Everyone is a hypocrite and a liar. Well, I'm not a liar.

Christ. Ahem. I think I should have a cigarette. I just did. Some tar for your virgin lungs.

Where was I? Ah, yes. We've all been checked into the hotel. The Hotel of Life! The Life Hotel and Casino! No clocks! Pumped-in oxygen and free drinks as long as you gamble!

"Welcome sir, may I take your luggage?"

Yes, yes.

"Your room number is the number of the beast: your wife! And dinner is at seven in the main lobby, twenty-five years from now. I'm sure you'll want to freshen up."

I've got to stop the smoking. The smoking.

7

I insert my Carl Philipp Emanuel Bach disc into the little machine. The music fills my head. Let's see. More snow is on the way, the cat stole a pork chop at dinner, and I bought three pairs of pants for thirty-four dollars. Also, my tax return should be coming soon, and we found a nice restaurant right here in Vergennes.

Moreover, Cubism lives in government, I am Virginia, and my left foot is bigger than rockets. Oh, and hurray for math, and let's all join the Masons.

8

Volume Five. My throat is hoarse. I think I'm sick again. DON'T DISTURB ME WHEN I AM THINKING, WOMAN!

God almighty, Mother of Satan! Great Whore of Babylon in my pants! Aughh! *Mooooonlite in VERMONT!* Sinatra! The Sands! Her tits at eight!

Oh great breast of mercy! Come down that I may drink from your fountain of delights! Genie! Blondie! Luck be a Lady! I have a dream! Education! Pigtails! An American queen! Venus of Urbano! It is Charlotte and no other!

9

Tomorrow I have to take the trash out. It's getting to overflow level. The cat takes the long way around the kitchen. And our little brown bags of recycling. Amazing how much of it you collect. Residue. Afterglow. Signature.

10

Females. Amazing creatures.

11

Across the street a ways down the road, there is a large, handsome, red-brick Catholic church with a tall, silver spire and a statue of the Virgin Mary out front. Here in Vergennes. I always look at it as I am walking by. In the evening, they have a light shining on the statue, and occasionally I walk up and stare intently at her face. She's attractive. Her face is staring down, full of softness and serenity and compassion. She's always there. Just standing there. Not looking very feminine, but yet obviously feminine. It's the body language. You know how they do up all the Biblical personalities. They always borrow the Greek tricks and give this otherworldly transcendence to their features and their expressions and their postures and their bodies. They do this on purpose. But I like this one. I like this particular Mary. I'm attracted to her. She looks like you should take her in out of the cold maybe, and invite her in for some tea or a drink or something. (You see what this state does to you, as you stand in the snow looking up at Mary?)

She's always out there every time I walk by. Out there on the lawn in front of Saint Peter's of Vergennes. I suppose I should go in there some time and see if the interior looks as good as the one in San Miguel. I find myself attracted to so-so, average, ordinary churches. Not the large ones or expensive ones, but the ones with simplicity and grace. The ones that are a pleasure to sit in. Same thing with houses. And women.

But yesterday I went inside. Yes. Saint Peter's. Walked right up to the main entrance. The doors were wide open. Luckily, not a soul was there.

Everything was just as I expected. Charming and subdued and cozy, all at the same time. Done up right, but not too flashy.

Yes. I stood in the entrance for a while. After about ten minutes scanning the ceilings and walls for hidden cameras, I wandered inside and into one of the confessionals. I couldn't resist. Of course, once I was inside and sitting there with the door closed, I couldn't hold back. I looked up.

"Forgive me Father for I have sinned."

Auuughghhhh! Haaaa! Ah God. Hilarious! It was the most enjoyable thing I've done since I moved to Vermont.

I sat there for several minutes imagining all the poor sinners who had sat inside over the centuries, spilling their guts about everything under the sun. I was thinking what a masterful psychological lever this was to pull down. How cleansing and rejuvenating. I kept sitting there, thinking of all the moments that people had spent sitting at this very spot, and then imagining what the good Father had said back to them. Wondering if things ever got really juicy. If he ever got to hear anything extra good. Something that required more than just a few Hail Marys.

Eventually I stepped out of the confessional and quietly closed the door. I made my way down the aisle, pausing every once in a while to sit quietly in a certain section of a pew. I flipped open hymn books here and there. I walked out to the side of the church where I could take in the paintings, one by one. They seemed to increase in size, force, and spiritual intensity as I moved slowly forward. Forward finally to . . . *the pulpit*.

Yes. I couldn't resist. I approached from the left and walked up the red carpeted stairs. Now I was inside the holiest of holies! The inner circle. I approached the captain's chair slowly. I looked up at Christ, and then one last time back out to the pews to make sure no one had snuck in. Quite alone I was. A few more steps and I approached *the chair*. You know the one. The one you've always wanted to sit in but have never been able to. Oh but now it was mine. Yes. My heart sped up. It was right there in front of me now. At long last. *The chair.* Yes. I reached out to touch the armrest. Real art! I felt I was floating. Time stopped. I looked up one last time. Up at all the angels. I turned around and faced everyone. Yes. Epicurus, Li Po, Nietzsche, Emerson, others.

I finally sat down. I took in everything. My heart raced faster. *The chair.*

Yes. The afternoon sun was filtering in through the glass. I looked around. I began to smile. I began to smirk and snicker.

Gradually, I adjusted to my new surroundings. The atmosphere inside the church began to take on the faint hue of reality.

Finally, I began to relax. I understood the lure. The power!

I began to imagine a ship. My ship!

"Row, girlies! Put your back into it, you ninnies! I said ROW! My daughter can row faster than that! Row, damn you! Are we taking ballet lessons? You little teacups! Are we learning to knit? I said ROW!"

I thought of the priest sitting there in a service. Waving something smoky and feeling connected and complete and sacred and empowered. I thought of the pharaohs. The Pharisees. And here I was. I sat there. Looking out over the congregation. My congregation! My congregation of no one! It was all perfect.

I began to imagine all sorts of things. Greece. Rome. China. Japan. A parade of virgins tempting my free time. Various scribes, translators, officers.

"Yes, yes. See that it's completed before the dry season!"

"No, no I won't be able to attend. I will be in my library for the remainder of the day. See that I am not disturbed except for dinner."

"Yes, yes of course but not right now. I am going for a walk in the gardens. I will be there for the rest of the afternoon."

"Burn everything. Show no mercy. To anyone. Well, except the females. But don't destroy too many of the sculptures, if you can help it. And the drawings. Never mind, I'll go myself."

I sat there for six or seven more minutes. Silent. Transported. Electrified.

Eventually, I had to leave. I suddenly thought of what would happen if someone were to walk in and see me up there. Most unpleasant. I took one last look around. I sighed, got up from my throne and walked down the stairs. I walked back down the aisle, soaking it all in. I turned around and looked up at my throne one more time.

I walked outside nonchalantly and back onto the sidewalk, looking carefully around to see if there was some old bat walking hurriedly down the street toward me with a phone to her ear. I began to think of reasons for my visit. Excuses. Things to explain to someone in the event I was questioned. Small towns are like little kingdoms. With tattletales on every corner.

But everything was unchanged. I kept walking. The sun was still out.

I began whistling. Snickering.

12

April 9, 20___. Burlington, Vermont.

Have moved residences again. Finally everything is done again.

I live in a condo now in Burlington.

The ridiculousness has begun and ended once more. I should be able to finally have a rental house to myself in this current perch. That's what my residences are, perches.

I'm up here in my room now. It's late.

I come in here to do communion.

Let it begin.

13

Dear friends: You of the Future. That thought-like future of strange living. Days of becoming. Permit me a letter . . .

You will think back to us occasionally. Yes! You will think back to us in your off moments. Your physical moments. Your offline moments. You will think back to us, of the dirt and the grime. We of breast and sperm, pleasure and pain. We outside ones. We finite ones. We of death and taxes! You will think back to how our days were spent as well. You will sometimes think that possibly our days were better, more fulfilled.

But concern yourselves not with such things. Yes. We go back and forth, we humans. We love the past and the future and even at times, the present. All years are equal under the sun. Yes. Don't forget. Beautiful animals do not question tomorrow or yesterday. But then again, you are possibly not beautiful animals. You have become something else, possibly.

Nevertheless, I envy you. I envy you as you may envy me.

O mighty future! Where will you go? Where have you been? You of the future, what is *your* future?

14

It is midnight. I sit here at my desk. I pray to the bringer of light. I flush again. (I'm sick with the flu.) A galaxy appears in the toilet. Light years across. Twirling away! Time speeds up, stops! Einstein pops up for a visit. Monkeys on the typewriter! $E = mc^2$! Superstrings! Dark matter! Hawking's wheelchair! Clocks ticking! Attacking! Augh!

Existence is . . . a Spiral. If the spiritual trajectory of humanity could be mapped out, the collective journey would be in the shape of a Spiral. Culture? A Spiral! Religion? A Spiral! Technology? A Spiral! The human spirit? A Spiral! Everything? A Spiral!

15

The secret to anything is to begin. Or in this case, to laugh. I'm sitting here and the day seems to be Saturday and I bask in my free hour of time as if all the years I've spent here are just beginning.

I'm looking out the window of my apartment down at the river running through the field below me . . .

Later on . . .

The cat is on the shelf in the kitchen.

I'm sitting here looking at my little globe. I'm looking at Mongolia, Burma, Laos. All these places and shapes and lands on this little sphere in front of me. A mild, hazy, five o'clock shadow, practically microscopic.

It's after midnight. It's started raining. The beauty of life is that it gives you days. It always gives you more days to try and fix your problem or repair your mishap. To mend your fence or sharpen your sword. Yes. For a while, quite a long while actually, life lets you roam and stroll and snooze. For weeks on end. Always days and more days. Sometimes life is simply this. This strolling through the castle to fetch pints of ale.

But it is spring! Yes! At last! The fields are green and the sun is warm and cozy yellow! The snowdrifts have receded for the season. The fireflies come out at night now. And the meadows. Oh . . .

You see how it gets. One day you're drinking whiskey with the ladies of the night, and a few years later you wake up living in dream land.

I couldn't care less. I sit here and snicker and look out the window of my latest abode. I look down at the river below, intently studying maybe, something idiotic and a complete waste of time, like, a bird or a duck or a cloud or something.

Yes. We arrive at a point finally where different things hold our interest. Silly things. A human spirit does not need new people always as it climbs into a ship and gives chase to new definitions of sentience. As it pursues higher forms. As it becomes slowly and surely, through trial and error, mistake and triumph, more and more and more!

I'm up here again . . .

Sooner or later, I calm down. A few hours later, I awake. Everything is quiet. I can hear water, a small fan buzzing.

16

It's about 70 degrees outside. The wind is blowing slowly through the trees. I can hear the leaves rustling here and there against the building.

It begins to rain again. Very easy, soft, very pleasant.

My life up here in Vermont strikes me as temporary.

But the land here is mature, fertile. The rocks seem alive. The soil, rich. The waves out at the lake lap blue at your eyes.

Music. Wine. My mind. Most things on a Wednesday. My brain runs twenty-four/seven generally, now. Calculating behind the haze, but slightly anxious. That's why writing is better. Yes. You can just let the *mind* take over. Feed it directly into something. Just hook up the hose.

I want a cigarette but I've sworn them off until I get my heart and lungs checked out. Currently, I am waiting on this stupid bitch at work to send me the forms. Nevertheless, I crave cigarettes nightly like I crave marijuana and coffee and sex. I crave so many delicious things. It is a supreme pleasure . . . this losing of oneself in pleasure, two or three different kinds of pleasure simultaneously. Spiritual, physical.

What is this place that I go to, that I need? I try to make it last forever each time.

But my summer is separated already. I sit and fret about it. Visitors have already lined up! Yes! I am selfish with my time. A tyrant. I can't help it!

It's the winter. After the winter, your body and your mind stumble out into the sunlight, finally golden. Hot and laughing. Yes! A day!

The most interesting thing about time is that you can take old mental walks to go to new actual places. It's one of the benefits of being out of sync with the zeitgeist. This tendency is in fact the reason we are out of sync with our times. This tendency for Cubism. For continuous multiframe viewing.

17

Yes! What grace! What majesty! What stellar cartography! Yes!

A clean, healthy, Epicurean world view is essential for viewing reality correctly. That is to say, with warmth and science, and a certain amount of laughter and awe. And there's always the arts. Females. Health problems. You see how it all gets mixed up.

But in spite of everything, there remains the joy in the magic of life: that little flame that flickers in the darkness . . .

But I can't seem to get excited about what happens in my own life, at least with regard to any sort of career. I have no ambition. I have only the noblest, most worthy ambition: sanity!

I submit there should be a new destination, a new salvation for mankind, one that does not change with the seasons. And what is this? What is man's destination? Spiritual health. His purpose? To cure himself. Of what? Of mental conditions.

Yes. If Rome can survive incompetence at the national level, so can America! I feel refreshed anew at the prospect of this. If it is true that time eats its children, then these present ones will be especially enjoyable for him.

But we here in the bowels of the earth cannot concern ourselves with such wastes of our precious energy. We have fires to stoke, coal to shovel, engines to watch. It's only in environments that offer you no respite that you occasionally go a little cuckoo.

What could be better than to exist? Than to live the "I don't know"? The "Yes"? The "Okay, but I'm still buying a pistol"?

18

Oh, Vermont. Summer. Golden days, rainy nights. Lightning. The occasional firefly. My only urge in life now is to purchase a cottage by a large body of water . . . complete with a little boat of some sort.

The great thing about Vermont is that nothing ever happens. It's frozen in time. The inhabitants are occasionally suspicious of outsiders, occasionally ill-tempered, but capable of immense kindness and charm. Basically, Vermont is a religion.

19

My girlfriend is coughing in the other room. A visitor has come and gone. It's been six days.

We live at 42 Borestone now. Yes!

I purchased a bicycle yesterday. I paid thirty dollars for it. Charlotte noticed it and told me about it. It's brown. Very basic. It's beautiful. Slightly noisy. It has a rear-view mirror. It's perfect. She even went and picked it up for me.

Yes! This evening I spent about two hours riding along the Burlington bike path out by North Beach. It's a little recreation area. I rode there and back. Pedaling along absentmindedly, watching the sun set over the lake. Lots of people were out.

Some French girls were laughing at my bike one time, so I smiled at them and looked down at their hips.

20

Fortuna! Woman of All and Everything! O Nature! O Prostitute!

What is this monster, this thing that we live in? This thing that produced volcanoes, minerals, blood, light? This earth that formed amethysts, labia, pomegranates, machine guns, these myriad forms of matter? This place that has always created. That will always create. This Möbius strip! This serpent that eats itself!

One day, more than likely there will be a completely different type of reality, a completely different type of matter. Just as we enjoy the miracle of life in a certain way and on a certain psychological wavelength, so too will entities of future eons enjoy their particular type of consciousness . . . as entropy takes its toll, as entropy works its magic!

What strange places await us? What moonlit nights?

Since the beginning, we have moved outward and upward and downward along an ever-widening arc of mistake, death, triumph, trial, and error toward versions of ourselves. Even with the intersection of say, a golden age, mankind still has to keep going past it and make a full circle again before it can be taken to the next level, upon completion of the next revolution of the Spiral. Many of the same type of mistakes are made. Eternally. This is paramount to understanding reality. Just because an intersection has been reached, it does not mean that a year or a century or a millennia of review or dissolution or destruction must not take place again before the next revolution can take you to newer heights on that same line still, as the journey continues on toward the next point along the spiral. Life is not an eternal recurrence of the same things; life is the eternal recurrence of different things moving outward along the spiral. Life is the eternal Spiral. The eternal revolution. Toward what? Ourselves. Truth does not evolve. Truth revolves. We simply look at it from different angles as time goes by. We experience it from different angles as time goes by. As we move further out along the arc, the eternal Spiral.

21

Here I am. Drinking coffee. Needed a little pick me up.

My intent is to distance myself from everyone. Currently I am suffering from Closeness Aversion Syndrome. Feel slightly suffocated and hot. The proximity makes my blood pressure rise. It is due to a spiritual hypersensitivity to other people's personalities and inner qualities that causes a shudder whenever my life starts to become too intertwined with theirs.

We wake to sleep. Life is noise and motion. Planes. Cars. Stereos. Bass. Treble. TV. Other people. Heaven and hell and other people! Heaven and hell and other people! Heaven and hell and other people!

One gets like this sometimes. I think it will pass as usual. Loss of appetite. I wish I could smoke marijuana and cigarettes all day, but I've had to give them up pending more test results that my new doctor is running. Maybe forever. It's a drag. So I've been drinking more. It's my only escape, besides Wagner and Debussy and Ravel.

What is the essence of life? Desire. A desire for more life. Or conversely, a desire for less life.

No? Ask a bird in a cat's mouth what he thinks.

22

Charlotte and I got high for the rest of the summer. Fall too.

Winter is on its way. A light snow fell yesterday for an hour or two. We sat watching it. It disappeared when it hit.

23

I'm sitting here at my old decrepit Hewlett-Packard machine. My Command Control Console. It was used when I got it. It was a gift from Bern. Now it's four or five years old. Not out of date, but certainly a long way from top of the line. But who needs top of the line, anyway? Top of the line is high-maintenance. I like my old, broken-in H-P Pavilion. Four years old at least at the time I am writing this. Serial number N-3402.

I'm sitting here drinking tea like an idiot. Everything seems to have passed into oblivion.

It's almost 1:00 a.m. The last few days have been awful. Nonstop. Always doing some bullshit. The oven's broken. The landlord keeps stopping by to get boxes out of the garage. All this bullshit. Day after day.

The great pageant of existence. It's glorious.

24

Everything has shifted once more. It's always becoming something else.

Yes.

We set sail for horror, across the flame and drifting fire. We sludge past on deck, clinking in unison. Amber corpses, navigating hell.

25

We've just arrived back from Woodstock. Woodstock, Vermont, that is. It was Charlotte's birthday. Yes. We had a decadent evening at Charleston House Bed and Breakfast interrupted by a three-hour smoke session in our Jacuzzi and a seven-course dinner at Prince and the Pauper. Marvelous! Yes. I decided to blow some money. And why not! Any day now, *something* is going to happen and probably lay waste to us. Or maybe not. At any rate, I can't resist blowing some hard-earned cash every once in a while on some meat and wine. And a lovely fire in a lovely room. What could be better?

And I must mention the royal service we got from the waiter with the Austrian accent at Prince and the Pauper as well. I went for the Thai mussels, the filet mignon, and a nice pinot noir. Also the mixed field greens and a chocolate torte. Charlotte had the pork and sherry. Naturally we went for some coffee as well. Ah, but the real universe happened later on in the bathroom Jacuzzi with the pipe. (We kept a towel under the door.) Splendid.

I can't stop smoking marijuana, at least not completely. But I have managed to hold off cigarettes for some time, although not without some considerable expenditure of willpower, to say the least.

I kept picturing myself living in Woodstock as we walked around later. Living out my days in some pretty, silly, little village like that and immersing myself in the charm and the snow and the architecture and the small vision of happiness that it is.

Unfortunately, the prices around town force you to realize that other people with much deeper pockets than you will ever have already had the same idea.

26

I'm laying here in bed. The cat runs in and stares at me. It's raining. The streets are tired.

I'm laying here in bed.

27

It's the end of the year again. I've become a crank. I snicker to myself.

I'm sitting here watching the snow fall outside. It's blowing sideways.

I'm sipping my tea. The flakes shift and dive in the wind. Every once in a while the building creaks. It's fascinating to watch.

I spend life traveling to and from the conduit. The confluence. The conflux. The la-la land of euphoria introduced by THC.

When you live here, life is different. People don't understand that you're on a different schedule. You have a different conception of time, even. A different experience of time. You have simultaneously much more of it and much less of it. It's a trade-off. You give up something in order to have access to something else. But in my case, it's becoming permanent.

28

January 20___. It's here!

Charlotte is out having dinner with her friend.

I've completed the first part of my medical checkup. Oh yes! The company I work for got sold. Bern gave everyone a small bonus and then, adios! But strangely enough, we have the best insurance around, now. Yes! Amazing how the luck can change, out of nowhere, presto!

Oh, but the doctor visits. Yes. Finally I have a legitimate medical diagnosis made that silenced my paranoia. Yes. Finally I persuaded a Dr. Sandy Bergman to get an ear, nose, and throat specialist to take a look at my throat. After a series of examinations, he pronounced my throat "completely void of any type of cancer, sir." He also gave me a lecture on marijuana and cigarette smoking, both of which I unfortunately enjoy immensely. I seem to have been suffering only from various stress or anxiety-induced symptoms. Brilliant! Now the only other thing is the chest pain. Ahem.

29

What is my vision of the world? The metric system. Typewriters humming. Girls in sweaters.

30

The good and the gracious. All the writings of hell. Thumbnails and poems. Slippers for the devil.

The days are wisps of incense. The nights are all forgotten. It's delightful. All I've ever wanted is coming true. Anonymity, dear brother and friend!

Tonight I set sail for nowhere. A short journey of just a few weeks. Load the supplies! I needed a vacation anyway. In the upcoming months, I will once again be looking for a little house. I've done this all my life. Look for a little house. Just something to rent. A nice little place. It seems so difficult for some reason.

In the meantime, I've plotted a course.

Attempting to engage Solar Sails One and Two now. Half speed should be sufficient.

"Sails aligned and engaged, sir. Switching to auto pilot now."

Ah. There we are. What could be better?

I slip down below. Mix a whiskey sour. Put on some delicate little Japanese music.

I make my way up to the forward deck. It's past midnight. I turn on the skylights.

"Ahoy land lubbers! Adjectives are the future! Verbs and nouns and platitudes!"

"Early bird gets the worm! A penny saved is a penny earned! Can't win if you don't try! All's well that ends well! Win some, lose some! E pluribus unum! Tax, title, and license! Factory-to-dealer incentives! Some restrictions may apply! Contest limited to residents eighteen and over. Void for residents of Puerto Rico, the Virgin Islands, and Guam, fuckers!"

I fall over laughing. Spill my drink.

31

My neighbor is a fat, loud cow. Charlotte and I awaken every morning at 6:45 a.m. to the sound of banging cabinets in her kitchen as she prepares the massive amount of food required to keep her fat body functioning throughout the day.

I have fantasies of murdering her in some stylish manner, and then walking back inside my place, quiet at last, and lighting a cigarette.

I have as usual about two months left on my lease. Things usually always turn to shit for me with about two months left to go. I always almost make it. It's become the story of my otherwise meaningless existence.

I am Sisyphus, rolling his ball of noise up the hill, over and over into eternity. I've accepted this as my fate.

But last night was better.

Last night, I was sitting around thinking of the various ways in which certain people and certain world leaders could be murdered, a la the French Revolution. My personal favorite was to turn someone that needs to be murdered loose on a few acres in the Serengeti with a young leopardess. Yes. So young that she would play with him for some time before actually completing the deed.

Ah god, imagine the chase! Bringing them down like a gazelle in a cloud of dust, albeit it a very small cloud. And then maybe dragging them up into a tree about twelve feet in the air and consuming them! Ah God! Imagine the sight! An idiot being dragged by a cat up into a tree, by the neck no less! Ah God. The mental image! Why oh why can't it be done?

When I think of the universe and all that it permits, why, it's a crime! It's not our fault, this thing. I ask you, O Great Father Time, when you vanquish your other children, will you devour them before you devour me? Will they taste as bitter as me? Will you not enjoy them a little more? And what are you yourself in the final analysis, Father?

32

Land ho, bitches!

Pronouns! Protons! Prophylactics! Lower the anchor!

The clock strikes twelve. My favorite hour.

The beginning of wisdom is doing nothing. This has never been more clear to me.

Oh, and I almost forgot: My chest X-rays came back negative. Well, with the exception of a few abnormalities, that is. Scoliosis and a slight sternum deformity. Two possible reasons for chest pain.

I went and had a couple of cigarettes to celebrate!

Life swoops down, flutters, takes off again!

33

Early February. Winter drones on. It's snowing. It's snowing as I sit here waiting on Spring again.

I sit here in the sanctity of my home, where everything is sacred. My lamp is noble beyond measure. This air, divine.

My only desires are to eat and fornicate. Human interaction fills me with horror. Children irritate me. Although nice little girls who have some unique talent for common sense or the arts make worthwhile companions. In another life, I must have been a goat. Or a seahorse.

Time is treacherous. A betrayal. But alas, these are human terms.

The secret to life is the secret to death.

As usual, my girlfriend has come home and ruined my perfectly good mood. She doesn't mean to.

I've thought of employing her as a servant but it would never work out. She would look perfectly handsome as a French maid or an English governess, but she's far too unruly. Besides, she has a tendency for secrecy and emotional outbursts. Oh, but her breasts . . .

I keep reading in the newspaper of thirty-year-old female teachers being arrested for having sex with their fourteen-year-old male students. For the life of me, I can't see the crime in this, unless the teacher happened to be married. What a stroke of luck for the young maestro. Yet inevitably the young maestro always turns into a little bitch and has to go run and tell his mother, who in turn, smells money, and sues the teacher and the school board for ten million dollars to help her and little Johnny get over the whole thing!

Does this sort of thing happen in other places?

I've realized that most people aren't here. I think that most people do not actually live on planet earth. They seem to live somewhere else. I can't quite make out where.

Again and again, I advance. I retreat. I plot coordinates. Check maps. Note positions. Life strikes me as large beyond measure, if ever so small and inscrutable. The lust for it all, the smell of it all! The feel of it! It makes no difference what century you're in. The pleasure is the same. The predicament is the same. Each day is a curse, each night a godsend!

Life is beautiful, futile. Its eternity is that of a flame. When you stop to consider the origin of things—the universe, music, mammals—the brain is confounded. What set of conditions causes a universe? Moreover, what is a universe? I suspect that, as with anything else, if you knew the answer, then you wouldn't be here to ask the question. The definition of life is . . . asking what is the definition of life. Still, the mind wants more. One attempts to conceptualize things in terms of time and space. One thinks of an explosion or an expansion of some sort. Thinking of an explosion conjures up an image in which one is on the outside of some point in space observing the explosion. But in reality there is no "outside" of the universe. You are always inside. You can't get outside.

If you could actually go back in time, it would keep stretching out so that there was always more time. Things would keep breaking down and getting smaller and smaller. No matter how far you went back, the universe would keep adjusting to compensate.

In some future eon, time and space will produce concepts unimaginable at present. Somewhere on the giant waves of time, we will one day exist in some entirely different state with some entirely different aim. With some strange purpose arrived at by equally strange means.

Time is a trick. A dream. A dog's ice cream.

34

Saturday. Charlotte is at work. Snipping away at locks of hair. She is a certified hairdresser now. She and her sister, both. Yes. She graduated from cosmetology school. That's what she's been doing with her time here in Vermont. She got a raise last week.

Oh, and I put down a deposit yesterday on a rental property. It's in Burlington's version of the suburbs. It's a tiny, plain, white house with brown and red shutters. Yes! It has a basement and a gas fireplace and a large backyard with a high brown fence.

I keep changing residences. I've moved seven times in the last seven years.

But I can't wait to move. I can't wait to waste the weekend once I'm done. To sit in the garage, drunk. I've decided that I will need to install a cat door at the entrance of the basement. Yes. I forgot to mention. The house has a basement. Perfect for laboratories, 1940s radio programs, experiments in sanity conducted late at night.

And it's stopped snowing finally. We've had three storms in a row. Now it's beginning to melt a little. This won't be good for moving. I'm always moving in the worst weather imaginable. It's my own private curse. I can't shake it. It always goes from cold to worse. Colorado. Vermont. The North Pole. Next up, Antarctica. Neptune. Pluto.

35

I consider the Apostle Paul. Yes! Listen! I'm struck by his mental fortitude. I admire him. But I can't forgive him for being wrong about things. And this concept, what is this concept of three days that appears so many times everywhere? Paul was blind three days. Jesus rose from the grave after three days. Father, Son, Holy Ghost. The three Greek Muses. Three days in the Underworld. The three hags. The Hindu triumvirate. Creator, Destroyer, Protector. Brahmin! Shiva! Vishnu! Pompey! Brutus! Caesar! Wine, women, and song! Shake, rattle, and roll! Three strikes and yer out at the old . . . ball . . . game! Augh Ha! Ah.

How simply grand everything is. We are truly living in a golden age. Everything is so noble and far-reaching! So self-assured in its trek upward! Toward the zenith of its destiny! Surely Europe of old, and ancient Greece, not to mention those Romans, how they all must be turning green with envy! Oh the wonder of it all! The glory! The sense of purpose! The loftiness of our goals! The finality of our logic! The undeniable self-evident goddamn manifest destiny of it all!

I'm craving a cigarette.

But I'm tired. I've masturbated this evening away. Frittered and wasted most of it already.

There's something about humanity that irritates me. What is it?

It is my contention that animals are occasionally worth more than humans. That some animals have more spiritual worth, more spiritual resonance than some humans. That some animals have more character, more beauty, more art, more delight in their being than a great many humans. It is true enough. No sane person can deny it.

36

The only question left now is this: Are we malignant?

37

My days are sunshine and death. I've caught a cold. The house
is modest, run-down, perfect. We're all moved in.

38

Our lives. Flowers. Spreadsheets. Quebec. People give way to things.

Wednesdays? All in good time.

Maturity. *Mode d'emploi.*

Je me souviens.

I sit here in bed now. I'm always in bed. The cat has plopped herself down on the sheets as well.

My new house is a kingdom. I've had a million moments already. Unrecorded. Lost jewels, eaten hungrily in the night.

And to top it all off, Kian (the Irish—he visited a few days last week) left a bottle of 1999 Fixin. Domaine Pierre Gelin. A brilliant red, very balanced, very elegant. Very intoxicating. Very well mannered. A good mood waiting to happen.

Glorious silence! The miracle! The mystery! The why! The because!

It is finished.

I am now complete.

PART 3

1

The house is incredibly large. I've never been inside such a large structure. The basement alone is the size of a football field.

It's three stories high too. And it came with an oversized parking garage for my Japanese sportsters. In addition, the backyard includes a little faux-Greek garden with Pan and Icarus chasing Solitude and Nausicaa through a waterfall. Actually it's Nausicaa trimming Pan's hoofs while Solitude lectures Icarus about flying. Well, to tell the truth, it's Icarus lecturing Pan while Nausicaa and Solitude make dinner. Okay, fine! It's Pan, Nausicaa, Icarus, and Solitude watching *Faster, Pussycat! Kill! Kill!* All right, enough is enough! It's Pan, Zeus, Jonah, Einstein, Kurt Cobain, and Christ playing Carl Sagan, Nina Simone, Richard Simmons, Lawrence Welk, and Adolf Hitler in world championship doubles table tennis.

And now for the weather. We've got a low-pressure front moving in from the northwest at 10-20 miles per hour, bringing with it some free time and excessive ejaculations. It'll start to mix in tomorrow afternoon with this band of cold air lingering here down in the southeast, generating an occasional feeling of contentment as it moves up the coastline here. By midweek we should start seeing a few moments of elation mixed in with a lot more pleasure at the higher elevations here. The conditions are ripe for several more days of precipitation, bringing with it more slumber and possible addiction before blowing out of here over the weekend.

2

I've decided that doing absolutely nothing is the best thing possible right now. I stay inside frequently. Else I stroll calmly back and forth across the backyard. I let the cat out. She stalks birds. They fly off.

I am being careful in my new house.

Ah, let's see. Let's take stock of things. Is there anybody left alive? Nobody from the old days except old man Crumb living in France. Oh wait, is Norman Mailer alive? Ah well.

It's Saturday. It's raining. I look over at the calendar. The days laugh. I snicker as well.

Ah, the struggle! It's so large! So small! So insignificant and monumental! It's ludicrous! Pointless! It's the only thing worth doing!

My urges are overwhelming. My lust for things. Women are torture. Life is a candy cane.

3

Work is getting rather stressful. I have a bit of insomnia still.

Because I work from home, the temptation is to doze a bit. Ah, but the eyes. The electronic eyes. They can see you! They see the files opening and closing in the database. They see it all on the server. The conduit. The Central Command Unit! They can tell. Oh yes!

I keep jerking awake today . . . suddenly cursing. I amble into the kitchen and make a cup of hot tea. When you aren't allowed to sleep, you always want to. You'd give money just to drift off. It seems like it would be the greatest sleep of your life. And it would be! But no, you can't! Not allowed. Wrong time! But then later on that night when you are trying to bring on that same feeling, that's when the mind heats up, starts percolating, humming. Sleep is the last thing you could ever do, now that you need it the most.

It's ridiculous. As most things in life finally become. It's a battle. As most things in life finally become. The week is an adventure. Saturday, a shoreline. I gasp for air, curse. Ah god, the salt. The sameness. The ocean. The waves. Josephine, where are you? The days. The streets, a desert. Hope dangling. Dragging the ground. Like a rusted muffler. Like placenta. We collapse. Gasp. We didn't even want to come out.

But here we are. And we constantly think of women! It's a trick. Like addiction. Like pleasure. Like THC. Or large breasts.

4

Commencing tachycardia. Full speed ahead. Blood pressure slightly elevated. Steady as she goes.

5

I'm sitting here smoking a cigarette in bed.

War is like gravity. Peace is like gravity. Life is like gravity.

My girlfriend likes to sit up at night watching late-night talk shows. I hear laughter every once in a while.

The cat wanders into the bedroom, makes herself comfortable. I go close the door again. She's figured out how to nudge it open with her body. I close it back.

These little somethings, these little occurrences. All over the world. Like people. Vines. Everything wants to grow.

What do we really need? We need exaltation. Religions, like children, hold the promise of tomorrow, but grow quickly up to disappoint us. What does humanity need? Wise figures in government: King Solomon. Franklin D. Roosevelt. (Theodore as well.) Thomas Jefferson. The Florentine Chancellors. Confucius. Hammurabi. Caesar Augustus.

6

It is very late. Saturday night. The wind is howling. It is the middle of May, but for some reason winter has returned. Spring fell off the calendar and misfired. It is a bit strange. And rather unenjoyable. Heat waves elsewhere. Rainstorms. Bizarre heat. Bizarre cold.

But I keep sitting down in my chair. I keep turning on the computer and going to work every day. Logging in. Clicking away at my maps. As little revolutions still happen. As the animals laugh and disappear. As the hungry world spins away and away and away.

7

It's Sunday. The weather broke. The house is heavenly. I'm sitting on the screened-in back porch in the middle of the afternoon, slightly high, smoking a cigarette. Tachycardia. Euphoria. The sound of birds chirping in my ear. The fruit trees. The flowers. The sunlight. A bird alights on the ground. A moment passes. Another.

I pour another glass of wine. And then more birds land. Blackbirds, mostly. And in the trees as well. The sound of birds fills the air. Chirping. Singing. Squawking. Bianca (our cat) sits silently on the table. She's transfixed.

I sneak up and let her out. All the birds fly off. All except the blackbirds. They fly up into the bushes just out of range where they proceed to start shrieking at her. They sound the alarm. More birds fly in to land in the trees behind them, one after another. They keep landing every four or five seconds. There are twelve or fourteen blackbirds in the trees now. Bianca's eyes are motionless. Her little body trembles with excitement. They mount an aerial attack. Two or three swoop down close to her and then fly back up. She gets nervous. She's crouched beneath a bush, wide-eyed. They're all squawking. Another one flies in. She darts out suddenly. Up it goes. Screeching. Then the ones in the trees get down closer. They all start screaming. She's looking up at them. Suddenly she feels the numbers against her. She's young. She gets confused. Her tail expands. She runs back toward the porch. The birds taper off.

A few seconds later, she runs back out underneath the tree again. She is feeling cocky and excited now. The cackling and the hissing starts back up. It intoxicates her. The birds keep changing position. Descending to lower branches. Then back up and over. And then again. They're trying to run her off. Finally she leaps up at the bird feeder in frustration. All the birds screech loudly and fly up to much higher branches.

Kenya. Right in the backyard.

8

I send my writing off to New York, Europe. The rejections continue! I snicker. Look off to my left at all my *National Geographic*s. Back over at my bed. I write from bed now. I can't bear to sit up at my desk lately. It's become synonymous with drudgery and toil. So why not the bed, where I can sit and relax and let my mind fondle the moment? There is nothing I like better than to exist. Simply. Anonymously. Sensually. There is no thought that can compare with passing of the moments.

And what places the moments take us. What strange hours dissolve before our eyes!

Spiritual trajectory. Yes. This is our real interest. Our true fascination. The preoccupation with the habits, customs, and tendencies of various psychological and spiritual *locations* and states of mind is our hallmark.

Crowds offend us. Centuries disdain us.

History swallows us.

But we sit in our rooms. On our porches. And we continue.

9

Ah, the glory. The sleepyheadedness. The heat of summer finally here. Windows are open. The hour passes. A thought runs down to the basement.

I've divined that people here don't like my car, my little, pathetic car. Therefore I have decided to drive it all the more and to keep confronting as many people as possible with its presence.

These little games. These little battles with other people. These little wars. These single-finger gestures!

When people deserve their unhappiness, I enjoy seeing it. I enjoy everyone ringing the stadium to watch the wires of their existence being reset and reworked. These little happenings of fate. This sunlight. May it continue to shine out across the land.

Occasionally an organism permits itself the journey of exploration. It is much like the lifespan of a single individual. Single individuals eventually grow old.

It holds true everywhere. Occasionally a culture feels the need to defend itself and feed and attack, like any creation! It is not entirely uninteresting. Occasionally I enjoy the spectacle.

I enjoy seeing petty criminals receiving their just reward, I confess. Not serious criminals, only petty criminals for some reason. I especially appreciate the methods of punishment practiced by the ancient Romans in the Coliseum. The forced theater performed by thugs and thieves (excepting crimes of passion or personal defense) which concluded with the actual death of the convict through one means or another! How truly just and imaginative. A triumph of good taste! How anemic our own system seems when stacked next to it. We have no stomach for this level of justice. Therefore, we do not arrive at this level of justice. This level of poetry.

10

The heat! It's here! It's relentless. All of a sudden, the warm air blew in. This room. God, it's too much! I can't write in this heat! It's oppressive! It weighs down the spirit. Uses up reserve levels of energy. It's gone from Arctic to Sahara. I sit here trying to work up the Zen, in a maelstrom of heat and heavy breath.

Ten hours later . . .

Ah . . . a cool breeze. There now. The voyage resumes. The sails unfurl with appetite and urge.

The wind begins to blow.

11

The fact is, we see things all too clearly now. And who wouldn't, given the bad theater that the world keeps turning out to be? But I love it dearly. It keeps me going. It has the effect of causing me to press on even harder, with even more intent than before. The weeks pass. Bridges collapse. I laugh and demand more! Next bridge! Next century! Next gemstone and turdlet that the earth keeps coming up with! All the great lovelies, and all the low lowlies! The mishaps and the missteps! The beautiful! The sublime!

Do I say continue? With all possible certainty, yes. Continue until you cannot. Be a long-burning ore! A faithful alloy! Exhaust your fuel. Give the fruit of your loins, your heat, your essence! Burn off every last electron, kiss every last atom. Glow for the heavens like any good flame!

12

Home at last! We've been running errands. Home at last! The minutes beckon me into the room. First thing I do is sit and snicker at all the nonsense I've read today. God, it's incredible. The buzz. Like so many flies looking for meat. And not even knowing what meat is. Humanity and its predilections. Its preoccupations. It's too much. The onslaught of the information. The rush of the tide. Detritus. Soft drink cans. Bad science. No science. Bad evolution. No evolution. Meaninglessness. Juvenilia. Misinformation. Lack of information. Mental condition. It's perfect! As long as you have a processing unit that can handle it.

What they shove at you over the airwaves is diversion. It's designed to feed you while you keep buying products. While you keep turning a wrench. It keeps you going. It's grand. Majestic. Insect-like. Ah, the spinning, piecemeal adventure of it all! The glitzed-out, fifteen-minute carnival of it all!

Humanity now moves into its next phase. Ah, the phases. They never stop. Being and becoming, being is becoming! Janus-faced thing!

Technology. Pharmaceuticals. Artificiality made flesh.

The future is obvious! It's the past that is a mystery!

13

My girlfriend is in the shower. Life sits on the porch, drinks tea.

Admit it: war is necessary at our current level of spiritual evolution. Admit it! There is no debate. At our current level of spiritual evolution (or more correctly, at our current point on the Spiral) we have either lost or not arrived at the ability to conduct global human affairs without armed conflict.

War can be studied and dissected for years on end until one realizes that basically it just rearranges things and allows other things (new life) to occur. The fascinating aspect is when one begins to tinker with the idea of accomplishing the same result as the armed conflict achieves, only without the armed conflict. The same rearrangement. The same rejuvenation, the same empty slate. But you can't. You need death.

Given our current abilities, ending war is well nigh impossible anyway.

And who can deny the obvious pleasure at the thought of so many well-deserving specimens getting sent to the cleaners every once in a while? No one.

Shiva.
Always.

14

The days seem like little bursts of reality punctuated with attempts at sleep that last about four or five hours a night. I've been doing it for the last six or seven years.

What do I have but time? What is my most valuable possession? What can I never have enough of? It is time. It is my pearl, my jewel. It is the strangest, loveliest thing on earth.

15

My house. The ship. We are taking on water down in the basement. The hull. It's all the rain we've had lately. Yes. I had to lift up an exposed wire and put down a towel and fashion a makeshift table for the wire to sit on so that it doesn't get wet. It connects the washer and dryer to the fuse box up on the wall. Maintenance.

Ah, the hours, the minutes. I lounge on my bed. An evening's hours already spent. The stroke of midnight.

The room. The house. I think of the days spent living here already. The eternity that it's already been.

O time! Strange ocean! Marijuana. Strange friend!

16

It is true that I seem to drift off occasionally. More just a bit of a . . . vacation from things. Mostly down in the basement. I find it comfortable and cozy down there. I feel hidden. I feel secure down there, where I can think in the soft light. I experience the pleasure of anonymity and solitude. The ease of the minutes. The stretch of the hours. I look at the walls, the foundation. The hot-water heater, the cement. The shelves, the assorted odds and ends.

I have a little chair where I sit. Occasionally I amble around. Or pace. Or play with the cat.

The floor is smooth red and gray stone. Buffered off. There is some insulation. A large American Indian style rug. Odds and ends. Heaters. Dehumidifiers. A series of wall supports and the beginnings of construction for a bedroom, abandoned. A series of boards running from the ceiling to the floor. Very open and airy for the most part. Very appealing if the sun is shining down in the windows. But appealing at any time, day or night.

17

I'm thinking of retiring to Asheville, North Carolina. Thomas Wolfe's place. The Biltmore, etc. And the weather. That's what I need. A temperate climate. God, where's paradise in the United States for non-movie stars? Nowhere, that's for sure.

I labor on. Have zombie eyes. Sleep less and less as time goes on. Am becoming fixated on things. Obsessed with things. I need an Oriental woman possibly. Or a Spanish woman. Yes. I am sliding away. The connections are being severed.

Doing things seems pointless. Things like celebrating Easter or Thanksgiving. These things seem like a horror movie to me.

I sit late into the night, every night. I can't help it. I feel compelled to press on. Pearls of wisdom are scattered about. It just takes a little time to round them up each night. I must find them. Seek them out. And the atoms. I hunt for atoms. I swipe the air. I have a special knife. There are millions everywhere. They all must be smashed! And then cut! And halved! And split! And the truth must be extracted! Down to the nuclei! The quark! The boson! The nyet! Nyet! Nyet! Do it again!

18

I've given up smoking for now again. The pains continue on the right side of my chest. More than likely nothing. I've decided to continue the marijuana smoking, albeit in very limited amounts, and forego the cigarettes entirely.

I am also partial to sitting on the back porch and staring off absentmindedly into the backyard.

I avoid social interaction. Quite frequently though, and more and more often lately, my efforts have had to increase significantly in order to maintain the current level of anonymity and solitude. In the summer all the friends and visitors come out of the woodwork. Every summer it's an endless parade of visitors. It requires enormous effort on my part to hold everything together long enough to get back to my work and my *raison d'etre*.

19

Back in bed now. I think a day has passed. The grass grows. The robins sing. The sky yawns. I sit drinking table wine. The day begins. Ends.

Once inside, I begin evening prayers. I approach myself slowly. I approach myself with reverence, and not a little humor. One must know how to laugh. One must know how to laugh at oneself.

I approach myself on stage. Yes. We are in theater together. I walk slowly across. Inside I am laughing at the gift I have brought for myself. My eyes dart quickly out over the audience. The seats are all empty. A packed crowd as usual! I get nervous. A hush falls over the audience. I am getting closer. I approach his Highness. I pull back my hood. I reach into my pocket. I place my gift at his feet. The music has stopped. I wait for a response. Ah! Now he sees it! He bends over to pick it up. The old troll! He sees what it is. He picks it up. He begins to smile. A snicker forms in his mind. He begins to laugh. He begins to chuckle. All at once he begins to heave and guffaw and his little scrawny body shakes and convulses. He starts coughing uncontrollably. He bends over his chair. He's heaving and holding his stomach. Beating the side of his throne.

He keeps leaning over the side of his chair farther and farther until all of a sudden it tips over on its side and he falls out onto the stage.

I am taken aback. His throne lays there on its side, with him beside it, still banging the floor of the stage.

"Why Highness, your throne! Are you all right? Here, let me help you!"

He laughs even harder. He's heaving. He's on all fours, crawling away from his chair. He looks like a hyena. Or a large rat. It is an awkward moment. He's still laughing and coughing and beating the floor of the stage and alas, my gift is smashed as well. It was a recipe for success! Made of the finest ingredients. It was brought over on horseback. The journey alone took two weeks!

I help him off the stage. The curtain closes. Another great performance.

20

What do we pray for, we atheists, we pantheists, we offspring of the earth?

We pray for the luck and the Zen. The truth and the way. Our prayers light dark nights; our wonder, dim futures.

We rise and bathe. Our temple is a garden of silence.

Summer.

I spend my evenings riding the bike path along the shores of Lake Champlain. I meander on little side trails. Investigate new paths. You can follow it all the way south into the city. Eventually you come out at the park. The Coast Guard station. The boardwalk.

The boardwalk is a little strip of benches about 120 meters long where you walk past all the yachts and the skiffs and the pleasure boats all the way up to the *Spirit of Ethan Allen*. It's a mini-cruise ship, about 170 feet long. It offers pleasure cruises, sunset dinners, etc.

It's very pleasant to meander around the boathouse and the boardwalk and take in the lake and the fresh air and the people and the ducks and the seagulls.

Sometimes I lock up my bike and amble around. Find a bench. Sit and stare at the water. The Adirondacks. The clouds.

21

My lungs hurt. Soon I am giving up smoking marijuana for a while. I've already stopped smoking cigarettes.

Nevertheless I feel joy, contentment. I feel distant, elevated, warm.

Life strikes me as something of a riddle, something to be alternately fawned over and forgotten.

22

Weeks later.

23

It's been a while since I have written. Various things have needed attending to. What's more, Charlotte is moving out. We are separating. She is moving into her own apartment.

It is the end of an era. For the both of us. She had just turned twenty when we met. Our relationship was the Ideal. It is horrible and sad, and we are crying.

She is now twenty-six. She is like a young bird that wants to leave the nest and try out its wings. We both realized it. I didn't try to stop it. It had been coming on for months. Years, perhaps.

It is true that we still love each other.

It is better this way, though, possibly. She is free now to pursue her own interests, her own life.

Nevertheless, I am cracked and bleeding. The days and nights of us are burned into me forever. They will not repeat themselves with any other.

24

Weeks pass . . . hurricanes.

25

It's now the middle of August. I feel as if I am waking up from a dream these past few days. It is Sunday. The sound of lawnmowers fills the air.

I feel the stirrings, the pain, the change. My body feels fatigued but my mind is light, instantaneous again.

I've never been more resigned, more frustrated. I am locked in a great battle of mind.

I sit on the beach. Nighttime is the daytime. Daytime is the nighttime. You want complexity? I want simplicity. You want simplicity? I bury a corpse.

Back down to the water. Water is rebirth. Oh mother! Hail the great woman! Saturn shudders at the sight of her! I fall back on the sand. A great storm screams in the sky! A monster and a tempest! I shield my eyes! Oh, infant that I am!

26

Life seems dreamlike. Illusory. Transitory. A mystery. Simultaneously, it seems so dear and priceless and worthwhile.

I've regained my faculties. I had slipped away for some time.

27

My room, ten thousand years. My body, a season at best.

I have a ravenous, all-devouring curiosity about things. It is the reason for my current troubles. My hunger knows no bounds. I am like a whale gulping plankton. I hunger for states of mind. Conceptions of reality. I swim silently on now. I glide along the ocean floor. Night after night. Year after year. It is my home now.

PART 4

1

Tonight I open up a bottle of wine and pour a glass and salute Charlotte. Our eternity.

These days I drink Rene Junot. I do not mind it. It is very pleasant. Very easy. Inexpensive. Previously I was drinking Estancia and Rioja and some Bordeaux or other. But now I am on a budget. No more guzzling. No more sesame chicken and crab rangoon.

Flux. The dance of matter. Make way for the pleasure. Make way for the pain.

2

On my calendar it is 3409, second year of the sun. It is 1920. Inside my hut I prepare the evening rice, the opium.

3

A few of the leaves are beginning to turn colors, but most are still green. Fall is on the way. The air is still relatively warm. Summer lingers a bit more. It's going to be 77 degrees Fahrenheit tomorrow. At night it will be about fifty.

It makes for excellent bike-riding weather. I find that as I get older I am getting younger. Yes.

4

Tonight I rode my bicycle through the pitch-black darkness.

The sun had set but I couldn't resist the urge to disappear down a trail out by the Ethan Allen homestead. There was a tiny sliver of light making its way down into the woods, just barely enough to make out the paths. After a few minutes the light was gone. The path is a little strip of smooth dirt about a foot or so wide, with several more feet of grass on either side. It meanders through the brush, beside a little river, over a bridge, into the forest, and though a field, etc. Riding on it is a marvelous remedy for pain.

In the twilight, one must concentrate not to run into a tree or snag on a limb or a vine or something. The forest becomes a different thing entirely at night. It quickens the pulse. The imagination stirs, comes to life. Light and shadow come alive. Shapes take form, disappear. It is invigorating, somewhat frightening. All at once, you reach a little valley in the woods that you had forgotten about in the darkness. Yes. The bicycle rushes forward into the black nothing. The heartbeat speeds up. There is a split second of panic in the darkness. I strain to see the edges of the path. It reappears. I ride up the other side, laughing. I start breathing again.

5

Charlotte comes over still. She still lives in Burlington. She still lets me have access to her body. I'm addicted to her.

We have little visits several times a week. It's almost like we're still together. It's almost like the beginning, but it's not.

6

I tremble. Autumn approaches. I salute the summer with the same respect I would accord a life form with whom I passed many fine days and nights. This particular summer had been especially pleasant, even amid the stress and fatigue of everything. I want it to never end. But I look forward to autumn as well. Let the nexus continue. It is the dream of pantheists long gone. The urge of those still to come.

I will compile a short list.

Anaximander, Heraclitus, Democritus, Epicurus, Lucretius, Li Po, Montaigne, Goethe, Shakespeare, Spinoza, Fontenelle, Chamfort, Diderot, Schopenhauer, Emerson, Nietzsche, Freud, Celine, Walt Whitman, Henry Miller, Bukowski, Carl Sagan. The light and the fury. The glory, the hiss of fire, the failure and the triumph, and the light . . . the good cheer!

7

Agents keep telling me my writing is not commercial enough to sell. Splendid. I take that as a compliment. Saturn, triumphant as always! I can't figure out if I was born in the wrong country or the wrong century . . . or both. No matter! I've said it always. I'll say it forever.

I smirk and step down to the basement.

The cat always follows me down. Occasionally, just for fun, I will sit in a different spot. Way off in the back by the old heater and the chimney cleaner, where the lighting is poor. Eventually her head peeks around the corner. She goes into stalk mode and begins to creep up behind Charlotte's Christmas tree stashed in a corner. She carefully sneaks up behind it. The whole thing takes a minute or more. Out of nowhere, she charges and runs right up to my face. She slams on the brakes at the last second, jerks back, and takes off around the corner.

Such simple pleasures. Youth. Old age. Everything in between.

I sit back and the shadows come in. It is an interesting way to allow the minutes to pass, sitting down in the shadows of the basement as the day wears on. It is magical. I feel hidden. Free to pursue my thoughts, and they, me.

At times I realize I am done for. Finished. Still yet, I feel wealthy beyond comprehension. Banks cannot hold these treasures! Nor vaults this gold! O invisibilities! Gems undiscovered! Currencies unknown!

8

I'm on the verge of sustaining an injury to my forefinger and thumb from clicking the mouse on my computer so many times. This program that I use to draw the digital maps for my employer eight hours every day requires an incredible amount of tedious finger exertion repeated throughout the day. It seems to be some sort of carpal tunnel syndrome. But what to do? One must work. I shall mention it tomorrow to Dr. Bergman. I've scheduled an appointment to get a prescription to help me sleep, as well as a pain reliever for my headaches. You see what becomes of one.

9

Tonight on my bike ride I stopped at the large, red, iron bridge at the mouth of the river on the far north side of the city. On the bike path. It was late. Night had long since fallen. I had been out at the Colchester Causeway, stargazing. But up at the bridge it was much darker. I stood there, looking up. I kept standing there. I couldn't leave. The expanse of the night. The clarity. So many specks! So many little pinpoints. Close as a thought. Far away as a dream.

I stood some more. I thought of somebody else staring up like this maybe ten thousand years ago. A million. And then somebody else, a million years on. And then everybody. The stars. The years. Physics. The past! The future! Ah, too much! I came back.

10

I've been going for Sunday drives lately—provided that Charlotte and I don't have an engagement.

Today I happened to pick a dreadful stretch of road. Every once in a while on a Sunday I will, if the weather is nice, select a new two-lane road that I haven't been down somewhere in Vermont for a day of driving. Today's selection wasn't quite up to par. It was Route 15 east out of Essex. It was not ugly, but not quite as enchanting as I had hoped. Too many dismal houses and trailers everywhere. Too many businesses all on the side of the road. Hideous. Tractor-trailer rigs. Lawn mowers for sale. Some sort of drilling equipment. One eyesore after another. I kept trying to ignore it. Some of it was pleasant, but I grew weary of laboring on through the visual irritants. When you live in Vermont, you want castles. Meadows. La la la. Girls in low-cut dresses, clutching mugs of beer and waving to you on the side of the road, Switzerland, music playing . . .

11

The weather is getting chilly. Autumn has arrived. The wind picked up today. A windy, cold, damp sort of day. Perfect for sitting inside and considering the leaves blowing around the yard.

There is something fascinating about being alone in a house, provided that the house is not too large. Not an apartment or a condominium, but a house. There is something exhilarating about the completeness of it, the singularity of it.

How pleasant to reside inside the walls. The separation from the outside so complete! So serene! An hour passes. How does it go?

The house is a chamber. A pod. I am fascinated with being inside. I am insulated from the cold in here. How novel to look out at the wet wind of the day and be perfectly dry and warm inside a pleasant room with flames and sustenance, with chairs and couch and books!

I am struck by the good fortune of living in a time period where comfortable shelter is readily available. What a rare gift, to sail in such splendor! No more caves, no! We delight now in suedes, rare coffees, rugs. We put on music to soothe our troubled souls. A nice breast is never far away.

12

A lifetime has passed. I have no idea what's going on.

13

The wind is blowing. Big gusts scream through the wood of the house. Howling. Banging little things here and there. Knocking small objects about in the yard. Occasionally a gust will come up out of nowhere after a few minutes of silence. The effect is startling. I shiver, go check the windows, put on some tea.

When I was out earlier, the lake was whitecapping. There was a very light sprinkle falling from time to time, but not quite enough to get one wet. As I rode along the bike path, the autumn leaves were blowing sideways from one side of the woods to the other. The effect was enchanting. There was virtually no one else out. I kept laughing. The harder the wind blew, the harder I laughed. A big gust would come up and reduce my forward motion to barely walking speed and I would strain forward into the wind, cackling, blaspheming, bellowing resolutely at nothing. Straining squint-eyed into the wind with little tiny bits of water tickling my eyes and my face. Every once in a while, a wet gold leaf would stick up against my cheek.

"Aughhhhh! You will not stop me! Must go on," I laughed. "O Fortuna! Me thinks thou doth protest too much!"

The gusts were near 40 miles per hour at some points. I kept cackling. I rode on. Eventually my face got slightly numb. I felt a little crazed. Something about the wind. The wind and the leaves. The sound. The senses. The pedaling. Straining. The storm! I must go forward! Forward into the storm!

On I go. Yes. My noble two-wheeled carriage carrying me along, the slave labor of my legs supplying the energy. On through the tempest and out to the Colchester Causeway. The causeway is a little raised path over the water, trees overhanging here and there on either side. Brush is scattered about. It looks something like a painting. The causeway was once the bed of the old railroad line. Back in the day, this is where people sat and puttered along on their way to Montreal from New York. This is where they sat and looked at the mountains of Vermont on one side and New York on the other. Here they sat marveling at the natural beauty, the pristine wilderness, the tax write-offs.

On I went, pedaling down the Great Causeway. Breath after breath. Minute after minute. The wind was beginning to kick up a bit harder even. I pedaled on. Past the islands. Past the old bridge. Past the little murals on the rocks. Five minutes. Ten minutes. Fifteen minutes. Breathe in. Breathe out. Breathe in. Breathe out.

I could see the markers coming up at last.

Finally, with a great deal of effort, I reached the end. The total distance traveled was only a couple miles, not very far. The path stops about two hundred meters from the other side of the lake. The trail would meet another path and continue on but for a sixty-foot channel of water that separates the two. This channel is for the larger boats to have complete lake access.

I sat there for a while on my bicycle, one foot on the ground. No boats around. No nothing. Just the howling of the wind and the waves crashing up against the rocks. The trees blowing, pummeled by the gusts.

I looked around out at the lake in the failing light, taking in the Green Mountains on one side of the horizon, the Adirondacks on the other, the causeway curling back into the woods where had I just been.

The feeling was of an island resort town in the midst of a tropical storm. I paused to take in the psychological effect of seeing such a vivid picture of the elements' potential for destruction. The experience was rather invigorating. I giggled and snickered like a little kid.

After some time, I began to ride back. This part was easy, as the wind was now at my back and was practically pushing my bicycle along. I barely had to pedal. Mostly I just steered and looked back and forth between the water and the path. The wind kept howling.

Soon I was back in the woods. I made my way out to North Avenue. The storm was coming on strong now. I kept turning around and looking up at the sky, laughing. My hair was blowing. The rain was falling faster. I was getting wet.

I made it to my turnoff, my neighborhood. After about ten more minutes I pulled up into my driveway. The wind was blowing very, very hard. I was soaking wet.

I snickered again, hopped off my bike, and walked it into the garage. The rain was coming down hard. I stood in the garage and looked out for a bit. I wiped my face with my arm and reached inside my pocket for the key. I looked out one more time.

Ah, warmth and dry towels.

14

I awoke to the sound of the neighbors in back cutting down the trees that separated our two yards. All morning and afternoon. Tragedy! I'm laying in bed, disgusted. It's incredible what a lack of perception and decency most people possess. I kept telling myself as I was standing there in my bathrobe this morning watching the whole thing that eventually I would get used to it, but at the same time I couldn't help thinking how unnecessary and idiotic it all was, how typical it all was. There was a whole row of perfectly sized evergreens that made an ideal barrier between the two yards, in addition to providing a nesting place for at least twenty small birds that I would feed. The only thing remaining is a dilapidated, wafer-thin, patchwork fence that seems at least thirty years old and looks ready to collapse at any moment.

People have such a lack of instinct in these matters. It's disturbing.

No more witnesses. The prosecution rests, your honor.

15

It's raining again. I'm thinking of Charlotte. Her perfections. Her laugh. Her hips. Her ample bosom. Her pretty little feet. Her painted toes. She has very pretty feet and hands.

(She purchased my pen holder and globe, the inscription, my black chest, various books.)

That things end is no miracle, but that they begin.

16

It's mid-afternoon. Time to pour some wine.

The day yawns and passes me by. I lay on the couch with my hands folded, looking up at the ceiling. The room begins to get chilly. I go turn on the gas fireplace, consider making some tea, snicker at all the ways I come up with to waste the weekend.

Bills are stacking up on the desk. I ignore them until the last possible day. A pay stub sits on the counter. As I work from home, I've set it up so that my paychecks are deposited directly into my account. One less item of maintenance. Now only food and leisure are left. Now I can run mental experiments down in the basement with nary an interruption, night after night.

17

I spent a long time looking at Mars in tonight's sky.

Tonight, Mars was the closest it will be to the Earth until 2018. I was at my favorite spot on the bike path down at the Colchester/Burlington bridge. The time was approximately nine o'clock at night. The sky was dark. The temperature was about 45 degrees.

After dark, there are few other riders out, if any. When the cold sets in, the biking is even better, provided it's not freezing, of course. Yes. Tonight I put on thermal underwear, boots, and sweater and gave it a go. Magnificent! All the instincts come out. One feels like an animal. A cat. A predator. Possibly a spirit of some sort. Yes, yes, that's it. A spirit, drifting along in the trees at midnight. Invisible. Ancient. (I think the best things about being a spiritual entity would be the anonymity and the voyeurism.) I would be fascinated by how the current crop of humans were spending their off hours, what they were doing at home in the evenings and on the weekends, what television programs they were watching. I would sit right there on the couch with some popcorn and watch with them for a while. What are they doing in the study? I peer over a shoulder as someone balances the books. What novels are they reading? Peering over the shoulder once again. What ridiculous pap they would be reading! What the nature of their arguments were. The spouses sitting at the breakfast nook, having the same argument they've been having their entire marriage. Oh, and one can't forget the kids. Just what is little Suzanne writing in her diary these days? Oh good heavens! Absolutely sinful what she did with Billy last night! What's this? Oh, she's got problems, naturally. Let's drift into the other room. Good heavens no! Jacob is masturbating again! Quick, let's get out of here! Christ, what an abysmal household!

Ah, let's go outside and drift down the street a little ways. This looks like a good one here . . . hmm, what's going on in here? Looks like the mother is talking on the phone, and Dad is in the living room watching a professional sporting event on television. He's transfixed. I pull up a chair and watch. Looks like the referee just made a bad call. Dad's getting angry. He curses. I sit there looking at him. He doesn't appear to be a bad sort. Ah, the wife is off the phone now. She's somewhat attractive. She walks up stairs. I follow her up. She walks into a bedroom where an adolescent is playing some sort of video game. She asks him about an item of clothing needed for a soccer match tomorrow, and then exits the room. She walks into what looks to be the master bedroom.

She walks into the bathroom. I step back and turn around and give her her privacy. I peruse the room. Eventually she comes out and gets into bed with a book. Ah, my kind of woman. If I wasn't dead, I would introduce myself! Instead, I drift up and take a gander at the cover. A biography of Judy Garland! Go figure. I sit in a chair to watch her read for a few seconds, to get the proper feel for the specific magic of her face. I watch her for a minute or so, smile, and drift outside.

The shitty thing about being a spirit would be never eating. Of course, the mental and physical freedom would make up for that to a certain extent, but there would be moments, after a few years of roaming the earth, when you would want to sit down and tear into a thick chicken leg with some country rice and cheese, accompanied by a huge goblet of red wine.

I pedal on, looking at the trees. Ah yes, the night. The cold air. Mars. Andromeda.

I am—ah shit, my bike chain just came off.

18

November.

It's Sunday. The SS *Mood Swing* docks at a new night. The whole weekend was shot. I couldn't even sit down to write, save for tonight. O, for a cigarette or a week of five-star meals.

Fine, let it snow to the rooftops! Let the snow begin! Let it snow us all in forever!

I don't really write anymore. I just scribble down the ship's log. I have much more important things to do than write. What's writing? I have midnight gardens to walk in, planets to worship, eclipses to study.

*   *   *

Once more into the dragon. Once more into the thing that I love. A lifetime appointment. A labor of learning. I come here to laugh. I come here to sweat. I come here to feel the glow and the recurring ecstasy.

Each night is a sword. Each day is a hammer. In the furnace of existence, new thoughts are forged on the anvil of disappointment. New men are forged in the flames of life. For what is there but the hot furnace of reality?

And when the fire is done with us each time and the blows have stopped, we find we are not ourselves but some new kind of metal, some new kind of iron. In the dawning of a new day, we find ourselves capable of some new kind of truth.

19

November 21.

We head through the treacherous Straits of Magellan and turn east for the Cape of Good Hope. If the weather holds, I plan to take a brief sojourn in the backyard.

I carefully run a diagnostic on the instrumentation panel and take a hit from my pipe. I grab the conn.

"Ahem. Attention all hands. For the next ninety minutes all personnel are to refrain from using the lavatories and restroom facilities. A ship-wide decontamination maneuver is being executed that will require full use of the water supply."

I take a hot bath. I take my time. Eventually I get out and dry off. I put on fresh clothes and head back up to the bridge.

I walk up the stairs, look out the window, button my cuffs. It is a pleasant evening.

I consider my crew. Napoleon is the first officer. Copernicus is the chief navigator. Carl Sagan is the resident scientist. They are all skeletons. Together we've criss-crossed the universe. Ran circles around reality. Towed matter through time.

Presently, we sit down to dinner. Well, I sit down to dinner and they watch me eat.

"Mr. Sagan, you're looking a little thin. Are you eating well?"

Mr. Sagan laughs and lights a cigar. He's wearing a sweater over his ribcage. He always laughs. "Well, what's for dinner tonight, captain? I'm starving."

We all snicker like adolescents.

"Let's see here. A nice thick steak. Whipped potatoes with cheese and butter. A side of raw baby spinach leaves with Italian dressing. Also a side of bread and a glass or two of Burgundy."

"Excellent."

I begin to cut my steak. "What do you think, gentlemen? Should we head north for Gibraltar or maintain our present heading and go to work tomorrow?"

Napoleon pipes up. "I sink yu should go to werk tomorrow."

I take a sip from my wine. "That does seem like a sensible option. Copernicus?"

"Yes, captain?"

"See that we head for work tomorrow morning."

"Aye, captain."

20

Winter has arrived. The first small storm of the season just ended. Five or six inches of fresh snow blankets the ground.

It is pleasant and cozy but it has the same effect on me as would a changing of the wallpaper or new curtains.

Nevertheless, I anticipate taking a late-night walk out toward the Ethan Allen homestead tonight possibly or tomorrow evening and seeing if I can disappear down one of the meandering little paths that run down beneath the property and into the forest.

The miracle of winter is the strange stillness, the icy quiet that grips the landscape. There is an immensity and a stillness to winter that is intoxicating. Winter has feminine charm. It casts a spell upon you. It is enchanting for a month or two before it turns into something that is a bit less enchanting, a bit more deadly.

21

Anonymity, dear savior! How I worship and adore you. Solitude at last!

In the Swiss Alps of the mind, in the great mountains and valleys of the spirit, in the late-night hikes and forays to strange climates, one can experience the freshness and nobility that are still available in life. One can taste the fruit that still grows in high places. Breathe the clean dry air of possibility and chance. Up here one can escape the humidity and the conspiracy of God. The dank specter of guilt and creation. The "everything must have a reason."

22

Judgments pronounced on existence arise simply from view, from level of magnification. A simple shift in viewing magnification is enough to alter even the most hardened viewpoint. The slightest turning of the viewing knob will unleash a thousand new worlds of matter and perspective.

(And oh, for a telescope . . .)

23

I am slowly becoming more and more obsessed with the concept of cryogenic freezing as a means of escaping death and prolonging life. Yes! Listen! As a way of prolonging the inevitable, to be sure, but prolonging it all the same. The idea tickles my fancy. I contemplate it endlessly. I go over the steps, the slim chance of waking, the horror of waking, perhaps. Waking in a time quite different from our own. A nightmare beginning after only the first few minutes. The possibility of a lifetime of labor and toil, or worse yet, experiments!

Still, the idea keeps returning. The possibility of a different future. The possibility of different planets. Different histories. Different women. Different regimes. Different realities. Different government. Another life. Another century. Another time. Time itself foiled. Death thwarted. Defeated. Turned back forty more years!

And then the thought hits me of dying again. At the end of yet another life. A few decades pass. A hundred years. Or maybe just one. I collapse from some illness brought on by the freezing. The body doesn't hold up. Dying all over again. Different acquaintances. Or maybe none. Just alone on a hospital bed. Three a.m. The body giving out.

What are the chances of the whole process even working out as planned? Maybe just turning out dead in the chamber anyway. Dead there instead of a grave. Just an exhibit. A specimen. Eventually buried without fanfare or funeral in an unmarked grave and that would be that.

Yes. There is a facility in Arizona that seems reputable. Part of the chances of being wakened again in some distant future would lie in how quickly the fresh body made it into the freezing chamber and how much cellular damage had occurred. From where I live now in Vermont, the chances of this happening quickly enough seem speculative at best.

But still, I think on it. The idea has me in its grasp. It's ridiculous.

And too there is the thought of leaving people behind. Waking to no one you have ever known. All the memories and the pleasant hours of the former life all gone. In the past. A memory.

Would we even like it, living once more? That is an unknown. But the urge seems well nigh impossible to deny.

24

What America really needs is a villain. Everyone does.

Ah, America . . . America is the end of the rainbow, true enough. Canaan! Land of milk and honey! (Just make sure you have your boots high enough on your legs.)

Everyone in America is looking for a home. They are always trying to find it. They spend their lifetimes trying to find it. Go west! America is the crowning achievement of Western Civilization. The definition of America is "the Western" movie genre. The hero riding off into the sunset is looking for a home, too. But what he's really looking for is salvation. From what? Himself. He's looking for something to make him forget all the things he had to do to make it.

A thought begins to form in our minds. Superstition remains, but Man is done for. There is nothing now but the hum of the artificial. Bring on the artificial!

25

What do we endure? What do we worship? What do we curse and love? The mystery. The "where does it come from." The "where does it go."

It is this strange, holy thing, this unknown thing that we endure, and that we love, and that we hold sacred.

This realization that life is a phenomenon is my Power Source.

26

Life veers and jerks. The pieces get misaligned. You stop and start in fits of mercy.

The days pass. Everything seems obscene. You feel trapped. Paranoia! Obsession! Compulsion!

Climate! Climate is what concerns us. After all, what animal doesn't need sunlight?

Ah, but the snow is here. It will be winter for the next five months.

I must engage the realignment mechanism. *Das Kraftwerk. Eine kleine Nachtmusik.*

27

I get into my tiny, green automobile and drive around. It is cold, but I drive around. The remainder of a minor storm is still scattered on the ground. Four or five inches of snow. Everyone in my neighborhood has their Christmas decorations out. Little sleighs in the front yard, lit up profusely. Candy canes. Snowmen. Little reindeer. It is rather pleasant.

I drive around. I have no idea where I am going, or how to get there.

I sit at a red light and chuckle. I am thirty-five. Single. Childless. No future. No past. A specter. A nonentity. A cell. This suits me. I look around at the interior of my car. Looking out the windows, I am more fascinated by the shapes in the snow than by any nine out of ten books or movies of the past year. I am becoming more and more disconnected with what most people would call reality. It's Vermont. Vermont is an experiment in reality.

The light turns green. I pull off. I realize that I need a young woman of about twenty-six to take my mind off things from time to time. She needs to be curvy and salacious, but not a flirt or a bitch. She needs to have ample breasts. Either European or a Southerner would be preferable, but not required. A Russian or Eastern European would be considered as well.

I drive on, thinking of females. I suddenly realize that my fantasy is now complete. Why change it? My ship sails on.

And temporarily, at least, the flame jumps higher. After all, what female wants to be subjected to a discussion on the origins of Lucifer! Or the English language! Or the toilet!

Ha! Possibly the occasional French girl. But there aren't any French women in the United States. Except a few in Manhattan maybe, or Silicon Valley.

Yes. I am Southern. I am polite, slow-moving. A little American. A crankmaster. A Crankmaster Deluxe, Model C19, Series 5, Special Edition. I am a misanthrope. An atheist. A pantheist.

I finally make it out into the countryside.

To Mad River Glen, and don't spare the whip!

28

I am debating the possibility of attempting to purchase a new computing device. My poor Hewlett-Packard is beginning to break down. The screen keeps going black. I have to hit the restart button for a second or so to clear the air. I have to do this several times a night.

29

Christ. The holidays. They wipe me out every time. They're over now. I've been having to read e-mails as well. To catch up. To make contact with what few people chance has seen fit to keep in my sometimes circle. I take calls. I do it out of politeness. Everyone seems hopeless. Everyone seems to live on another planet.

But I must not forget what important times we are living in.

I am now laying in bed, where I can appreciate the full scope of everything.

I am very glad that we have two opposing forces in America today. It keeps things in balance. Keeps things in check. That is, as long as one side doesn't accidentally tear a hole in the thing.

We've all become life junkies. War junkies. Political junkies. We want news! Always more news! Must be fed!

We're all stuffed. We're all starving. It's magnificent. It's ridiculous. It's a new kind of heaven. A new kind of hell.

30

Charlotte is moving back to Colorado in a few weeks. She has still been coming over to see me, and to let me see her. We have been sleeping together all this time. I can't resist her. Her flesh is so delicious. I will miss her the way one would miss life itself. She is one of the few women (and one of the few people in general) I've ever met who didn't play *chess* with things. I intend to reunite with her.

31

We yearn for forever. Forever is not there.

Having said that, there are few things better than watching it snow out the living room window with a hot toddy handy and a fireplace flickering in the background casting shadows on the wall. I am looking out now and the flakes are silhouetted against the light of the streetlamp. They are coming down in waves and sheets, alternately floating softly and then lunging sideways in the wind. Sometimes they reverse course and blow backward or climb up into the air for a bit and spin around in little miniature tornadoes. It is very soothing to watch it in the light at night.

There are already four or five inches of fresh snow on the ground now. It puts a new face on the neighborhood. Makes it seem softer, more graceful.

The wind is howling through the cracks in the house. Occasionally you can hear the pop and grind of material shifting. The cat gets nervous from all the noise. She looks around. Runs here and there to check on things. She looks back at me to check my face to see if I am concerned or alarmed. I laugh, call her over. (I've been weeping softly.)

"Noble kitty, come hither! Have some spirits! Toast the night!"

She runs off. Gallops off into the bedroom.

32

Snow Girl approaches. Hopefully, she will be wearing one of her low-cut blouses.

The cat sits licking herself by the fire. I've decided the publishing industry is spent. The Internet, too. We need something else.

Vermont is a cold-weather club. The winter here is a long cold train to nowhere. If only it weren't so enchanting, I would get off.

33

A day. My job. I sit glued to the screen, performing tedious, repetitive digital tasks over and over. Hunting down errors. Correcting them. Transferring files. It seems I am always catching up. Work is like a machine that has you in its grasp. I simply endure it and work as hard as possible when I am there and try not to think about it when I am not.

34

We lost. We lost the race. It's over. The final score is in. It's a wrap. Cut it and print it.

35

The Spiral. That bitch. I marvel at it. That is when I am not recoiling in pain.

It's like circling around the spokes on a bicycle tire. Various episodes of sadness and shit are repeated again and again as the Spiral crosses the lines, a little further out each time.

We have our lines. Our lines have us.

The Spiral: visual template for invisible things.

36

Winter continues. Today a fresh snow fell. About eight or nine inches.

I've been hibernating, meditating. It's fascinating, the completeness of the solitude now. The question of my continued sanity comes up for review. All concerns are quickly dismissed.

I pace. I sit and look out the window at my modest little neighborhood. I take virtual tours of various cities on the Internet.

On a whim, I decide to put on some warm clothes and shovel the driveway. (I haven't been outside in several days.) Snow is like spent love. Waiting to melt.

Shoveling took about an hour. I wanted it to take even longer.

I only smoke marijuana about once a week now.

I haven't talked to the neighbors in a while. They are elderly. Somewhat. They are very kind. The old man is a veteran. He loves to talk about convertibles. He loves to talk about riding around Spain in his MG after World War II. I immediately liked him. He's normal. He has common sense. He's not neurotic or boorish or overbearing. I feign ignorance and naïveté when we are all talking in the front yard. I relive his past glories with him. I ask questions.

Like I said, I've been hibernating. Repairing wounds. Regrowing tissue. I exist here, in this tiny white house. It is a mansion to me. A womb, a castle. The perfect place to reclaim sanity. The perfect place to lose it once again.

37

Monday. I take my medicine. I laugh and take my pills. I line them up. Patience. Resolution. Death. A good fucking time.

It snowed again. Winter howls on. The temperature is supposed to be about five degrees Fahrenheit tonight. The wind won't stop blowing. The winter plastic and the wood covering up the screen on the back porch keep blowing off. I have to go out and nail them back up. The weather is like fighting death on the high seas of nowhere, with only the cat around to watch. I curse, and get my hammer and nails and an extra piece of plastic from down in the basement. I open the back door and am greeted with the jolt of the cold and the wind.

I am Captain Ahab. Yes. I climb up the main masthead, the wind and the rain hitting me in the face, water dripping from my chin. "Auughhhhhhh!"

Lighting strikes. Thunder cracks down out of the heavens. The main mast splits in two right above me, and falls down, almost taking my head off.

"Auugghhhhh! God damn it"

The fallen mast crashes down onto the deck and shatters. A chunk dangles over the ocean.

"Aaughhhh. Jehovah's Witnesses be damned!"

I restore the plastic, despite the wind and the cold.

I finally make it back inside, teeth chattering, shivering. I stomp the snow off my boots. I walk up to the cat, let her smell my hand and touch my cold fingers.

"Yes, that's a good kitty. See how Daddy keeps everything shipshape and in good working order? See how Daddy goes outside and does unpleasant things for a good little kitty? Does little Bianca know that Daddy loves her? Yes she does. Yes she does. Oh yes yes yes she does."

38

I'm debating whether I should make some tea, or just hit the pipe and kiss off the rest of the night.

I went for a bicycle ride today in the snow. It was marvelous beyond belief. I managed not to fall down, although a couple of times I came close.

I was out on the bike path just up from North Beach, pedaling along in the white and the cold. Everything was even quieter than usual. This time of year the path looks like a long white tunnel with trees on either side. You can hear the snow crunching beneath the tires as you ride.

There were one or two other people out. Passing walkers while riding on your bike in the snow is interesting. I smiled and did my best not to hit them or slip and fall as we greeted one another.

After a while I decided to head out toward the Ethan Allen homestead.

The brutality of winter on the landscape is slightly fascinating. The cold hell of it all—the cold hell that it all could easily become if you were left out in it—becomes quickly apparent. One thinks of other creatures living in such weather for their whole lives.

But, it's oddly alluring. You find yourself stopping to stare at things.

I paused for several minutes in one deserted section of the path. You never appreciate what a bizarre phenomenon silence is until you experience it in a frozen landscape for an extended period of time. The combination of the two on the human mind is mood-altering. After a while, it induces a slight intoxication of some sort. Reality seems different. The forest begins to seem rather odd. If you continue on in utter stillness, you begin to notice sensations coming in on wavelengths that you were unaware of before.

It is during such experiences that a different type of knowledge flows into the mind. The span of the eons seems more easily grasped. The power and the spectacle of creation introduces your mind to different examples of reality. You realize you never noticed how strange and otherworldly the forest is. How you don't really know what it is.

I looked off finally. Time seemed to stop. All of a sudden, a lone little snow bird alit on a limb beside me. We looked at one another in silence. We stayed like that for a bit, trying to figure out what the other was up to.

I giggled. I knew nothing. I realized there is only the nothing, and that even the gods sit and wonder.

39

Tuesday.

I can't stop thinking about women. It was at the grocery store that I saw her. This strange girl. It's incredible how lovely the female body is. The shape stimulates instincts from back when you were a sauropod. You can't help it. The sauropod itself is just a complex manifestation of the concept of gravity. And what stops gravity? Nothing.

You can even go further back. Even the Big Bang is just a signpost of the mystery. The mystery goes on.

40

I pad around in my robe on the weekends. Drinking tea. Drinking wine. Drinking beer. Drinking coffee. Trying to get it together again.

Luckily, the phone never rings anymore, with the exception of the landlord calling to politely ask where the rent check is. I pay an obscene amount to live in this house. I am unmoved by it. I live like a king now. A mouse. A lord. A pauper. It stretches into infinity. I would do it a million times over.

I'm sitting here now in the living room again for a change. The room is very pleasant. I had forgotten how cozy it is to sit and type in the living room.

I've been moved to the point of tears by . . .

Hold on a second. Someone is walking up the driveway. A visitor! Heavens no. Ah, today is voting day here. Yes, that's it. Ah. She's out putting pamphlets in everybody's mailbox. Oh thank God. She's not going to knock. She's stuffing something into the mailbox now.

Oooh. A bit plump she is. One too many trips to Ben and Jerry's.

It's interesting sitting inside your living room and watching a stranger stand on your doorstep just a few feet away from your life and your privacy. Just a few feet away from the dungeon. The lair.

She is out distributing flyers. Trying to get us to decide between Debbie the Democrat and Rob the Progressive, and then there are the other candidates. The also-rans and the loonies. Yes.

Choice number three is "Boedy the Plowman." He probably makes more sense than anybody. But who is going to vote for someone who rants on public access and goes by the name of Boedy the Plowman? He sits there on his show—basically a radio show that happens to be on television—he sits there in his rocking chair against a live-action backdrop of cows grazing in a big Vermont pasture somewhere in the Champlain Valley and yaks about various matters for hours on end. Once I was watching him rant about something and there was a cow taking a shit just in back of him on the screen. Yes. He's off on something and in back of him the camera is trained on a cow's ass as it defecates voluminously onto the ground. I was sitting there taking hits from the pipe watching this. I laughed so hard that I thought I had injured my right lung. (Charlotte would have pissed her pants.)

Oh yeah, but the candidates. Number four is Royal Blot. Yes, that is his actual name. He is the other joke on the ballot. I was watching him "debate" on public access television the other night, and he actually made a point of mentioning to the audience that he was intelligent, that he wasn't a good test-taker, but that he was intelligent all the same.

"Why, thank you Royal. I'll be sure to remember that when I cast my ballot next Tuesday."

Number five is the token Republican. I can't even remember his name. I was snickering as I watched him make his points in the televised debate. He has about a snowball's chance in hell of getting even 10 percent of the vote here.

A tough choice, I'll admit. I voted one time in my life. Maybe I will again someday.

41

Sunday.

I'm sitting here listening to Mantovani. (Charlotte got me hooked.) I've taken to sitting here in the living room on weekends and staring out the window for several hours drinking coffee.

I'm debating hooking up the cat to her harness and taking her for a walk out by the Ethan Allen homestead. I'm wondering if she could have the good sense to walk that far with me and not just sit on the sidewalk refusing to move and trying to pull out of her harness.

I decide against it for now. It's a bit cold. Besides, she is snoozing by the fire.

42

I keep getting rejection notes from publishers. I look off. Go make some tea.

My only aspirations now are sanity and continued employment.

Failure is fascinating. Failure is freedom. It makes you more distant, more direct. It makes life more vivid. More intense. More 3-D.

I am honored.

43

Time passes. Still I sit. The room changes. I resign myself. Steel myself for future struggles. Future defeats.

I read books. It's useless. I attempt to sleep, wake up, work. Attempt to function. Life is a daydream. The circus never ends. Humanity is a nightmare. The eons evaporate. Things die. I cough. Look off.

I'm tired. I still chase the lightning. My clothes get soaked. I'm fatigued. Ah, the body. Health. I worship it. I want it. I need it! I will have it!

44

The temperature has risen just a bit. Spring is on its way. Little yellow flowers are growing in the grass. The beginnings of little buds are to be seen on some of the trees. A peak here and there.

Birds begin to sing.

I amble outside on the back porch. Bianca sits meowing to be let out. I take a cup of coffee and we walk out into the backyard, out into the sun. She immediately comes to life and sniffs around. I go get a chair from the back porch and sit down.

The sun is warm. The birds are chirping. I sit reading an illustrated book. The afternoon yawns. Time stretches out and stops. A fantasy of hours.

45

I worked outside today. The sun was magnificent. A few pleasant hours sitting around in the backyard, doing stray bits of yard work here and there. Laying around. Drinking coffee.

It occurs to me I am at the zenith of my solitude. If I were any more alone, I wouldn't exist. I am at the pinnacle. I look up at the sun. It's like a warm, slow breast.

46

I don't know what anything is anymore. I only know that I respond to stimuli. That I am stimuli. That I provoke stimuli. Outside of that, it's all beyond me.

Everything seems like a fairy tale, or a dream, or should I say, what everyone is doing seems like a dream. I, finally, seem like a dream.

Physical pain always realigns you with reality again though. It's then that you realize who and what the guard is that's been stationed there. It's then that you realize what it is that protects the sensitive areas.

People tend to disregard the body. It has taken quite a while for the Earth to come out with a homo sapiens body, a homo sapiens mind. Countless eons of life and death have passed through endless corridors of reality.

The putrefying stink of a human body is what holds the mechanism that designs lifetimes, that performs miracles, that lifts back the veil of time to map the constellations, and then journeys further still to the psyche and the mind itself.

47

I sit on the toilet reading the Book of Revelations.

I sit reading about 666, ("Nero.") Reading about the Laodiceans, the Great Whore, Babylon. It's all rather titillating.

The phone rings. I ignore it. My phone always rings at the most inopportune moments.

Eventually I give it up, close Revelations, flush, stand up.

It is finished. Alpha and Omega. I am the beginning and the end. For mine is the power and the glory forever and ever. Amen.

48

You can never go home again; that is true enough. Sometimes you even want to.

Spring is officially here. I sit listening to church bells, gazing absentmindedly out the window, as I am prone to. I look at the cascade of pink and green trees in the yard, cropped by the blue of the skyline. The mountains are in the distance.

I am high. An hour has passed. On a whim, I take out my credit card and order Chinese food. Sesame chicken, crab cheese wontons, etc. I go get a beer and put it in the freezer to chill.

My days are breaths of perfume, thoughts of lace.
At night, the ocean floor. Ping, ping, ping.

49

Yes. I think I need a systems analysis. I need to run a diagnostic. I haven't gotten drunk and thrown up in quite some time either.

The landlord wants to put a new roof on the house. It's always something. Disturbing my gentle Zen. The siding is next, he says, and probably the windows. God! Send in the 131st Infantry, why don't you? It's Normandy! Yankees at Tara! Christ! What next?

Yesterday I get a notice that the gas and electric is going up 15 percent this year. Only 15 percent?

You see, it's not that everything always changes, it's that nothing ever changes! Soon there'll be knocks on the door. Noises. Zombies banging on the house. Bianca will run down to the basement, scared. I'll be sitting there in the back bedroom at my desk, trying to work. My boss will call and ask what that noise is in the background. There will be a thousand interruptions. They'll track everything up. There will be various piles of trash collecting in the yard.

Every morning they'll show up at 8:00 or 9:00 and start beating and hammering. Walking on the roof. Ripping shit up. Ridiculous! Construction! Everywhere! Incredible. Ah God, the noise! It'll be eight hours a day! Insanity!

I find myself longing for winter again. For the snowdrifts and the solitude and the silence. For the wind swirling outside. For the two feet of snow to keep everyone nice and pinned down.

God, what's wrong with me? I gesticulate. Fall out of my chair.

50

Burnt sienna. Burnt youth. Supply-side economics. Sandstorms. "These are the times that try men's . . ."

We reveal ourselves in the offhand gesture, the unrehearsed response. Ordering food from a waiter. Checking on a bill with customer service. Making a turn on the freeway.

As one of the five remaining super-predators, what mankind really battles is its own id.

We sail on. The chains clink. Rations are low.

Occasionally the sun comes up. A bird shits pre-historically on deck.

We sail on through the boiling red, the thick and frothy ocean. A pterodactyl swoops in, screeches. I sweep the bones overboard and keep the shackles for spare metal.

My only friends are the foam of night and the spray of good luck.

51

I fall off a log. A raindrop hits. Somebody carves up a steak. Action. Reaction. Rewind. Repeat. Fast forward. Shuffle.

I seem misaligned. I read a magazine, think vaguely of a dream from last night.

Everything has become a foreign country. The passage of time is beyond my current capabilities. Most everything is. Empires rise and fall. Civilizations crumble. I sit reading a food label.

I'm slowly losing the ability to write as well. I watched a dragonfly in the weeds today for minutes on end.

I build pyres in my mind. Fumble around for matches. I have disassembled the various apparatuses in the basement and shipped them off for parts.

The weeks are meaningless. The days, excuses to breathe. I dream of women in gauze and white dresses. If only a ghost were present to instruct me on how exciting everything is in the afterlife! But alas, we are caught.

I sit and type rather than do anything that's actually constructive. This way I don't have to think. Frequently I fantasize about Nordic women clothed in animal skins. Or else some Victorian ideal sitting demurely in a parlor.

My lights get brighter and then dimmer, alternating mood swings of desperation and ecstasy. Everything I think is borderline mental condition.

It keeps raining and raining and raining. The monsoon keeps returning. It has stalled in the hypothalamus, along with my hopes for a literary agent.

Heaven never ends. I need only continue working.

52

I sit here drinking wine and eating chocolate for breakfast. The heat from the fire is very pleasant. I have it turned up all the way. It's about 75 degrees in here. It's about 55 outside. I am high.

The clock strikes four in the afternoon. Time for tea. Yes. Byron would have been jealous of my current lifestyle. Yes. It's beyond lazy. It's the lifestyle of an addict. I am derelict in my duties. I sit here snickering. I have no wishes. Only more of this.

All meaning has been murdered off, at least for now. All we have to do now is graze and manufacture new concepts.

The pieces of our train wreck are just the parts for a new machine.

Meaning and progress were temporary. Even democracy. The wheel creaks and turns, and we all end up under it eventually. The object is to get past this. Move beyond it. To take it for a spin for a while.

Don't worry, somebody will get in when you leave off. To them, it'll be new. This is the trick and the laughter.

PART 5

1

Shades of a New Epoch, the Open Volume.

The information overload continues. We're all hopeless now. Too much is not enough. Neurosis is expected. Pathology is expected.

I sit here drinking ale and nibbling peanuts. A primate.

Eternities pass. I yawn. My fingers are centuries. My mind is the years.

I sit here through death and torture. Through dismemberment. Whitecaps. Oceans.

It's all ridiculous. Life is a constellation of pain. Life is the highest art.

The backyard hasn't been mowed in three or four weeks again. The monsoon continues on. I laugh. Hyenas, lions lurk in the plains. Gazelles graze. A wildebeest gallops through.

The cat lays on the carpet beneath my feet.

I sit looking at my books like an idiot.

Dear friends, our minds are there for the conquering.

There's nothing left to want. We finally got *everything*.

2

Writing continues, life continues. I can't remember if it was Pocahontas or Sacajawea that made me laugh the most.

The oil in my car needs changing again.

The evening is always here though, to massage my neck, my back, my mind.

I sit up, scheming of ways to not work. I scour the Internet. It's a jungle. A komode. Television strikes me as being needed, but much more horrible than is necessary.

3

The fireflies are out now.

Tonight I rode over the Wetlands Trail. It's a collection of little wooden boards that meanders through the marsh for a little ways out at the Ethan Allen grounds. The path curves around through lily pads and pockets of dark green water with huge plants and vines and flowers snaking around everywhere. It's about four feet wide. Several sections of it are beginning to dip down into the water. Pedaling patiently along on a bicycle keeps you going just fast enough to foil the mosquitoes, but slow enough to enjoy the effect.

After dusk, the fireflies put in an appearance. They were going off like little flashbulbs. They lent a certain wonder to the proceedings.

The frogs and the birds started up presently. I continued on through the magic. Something large swooshed in front of me.

Eventually I headed out toward the fields and lanes that lead out to the Adams Public Farm and the Caulkin House. The fireflies continued to blink off and on.

Night fell.

4

The profound solitude never ceases to amaze and delight me. I sit here snickering and whimpering to myself.

We are left to our own devices.

I sample the fruits. I investigate phenomena. I swing on the playground. The buzz is exciting. The rides, the cotton candy. Everything is an amusement park. Who doesn't love forgetting?

There's nothing to do but have some fun at the amusement park. There's nothing to do but ride the merry-go-round. The roller coasters. Ah, the days. The summer days. The eternal days. The sunshine. The laughter. Ah, the laughter. The screams of delight. The thrills and chills and spills of the spirit. We jump from one to another. We chase one thrill after another. On to the next. And the next. Let the games continue! Ah, and the music! The wind-up toys! The shooting matches, the freaks and the giants and the one-armed man and the hall of mirrors and the water rides and the Lagoon of Death! The five-hundred-pound ladies! The fire-eaters! The snake charmers! The fun house! Test your strength! Bet on the little horses! *Ding-ding ding-ding-ding! Zap! Pow!*

"Ladies and gentlemen, step right up! Step right up now! Don't be shy! Come one, come all, great and small, far and wide, to the greatest show in the history of mankind! The one and only! The best! The greatest that ever was! Get your tickets now!"

Tum-tum dada-dada-da-dum tum-tum . . .

"Hey Emily! Let's go inside the fun house now!"

"Tom and Shelly went!"

"Hey Bobby, want to test your strength?"

"Hey Mom! Hey Dad! Over here!"

"Quick, let's get our tickets before the show closes. I want to see the Lagoon of Death!"

"Oh come on, can we please, can we please?"

"Hey Gene, let's go ride the Ferris wheel again!"

"Let's get a pretzel."

"Come one, come all to the greatest show in the history of mankind!"

"Hey Milo, I bet you can't hold your arms up all the way on the Cyclone!"

"Hey Maury, over here!"

Tum-tum dada-dada-da-dum tum-tum . . .

"Come one, come all to the greatest show in the history of mankind! Come one, come all . . ."

5

Sunday night.

I think of pomegranates. Picasso. Pompeii. I play with my two little paintings. They're not very good. I'm much better at staring off out the window.

I haven't driven my car in about six days now.

I keep hearing noises on the roof. I just got up and walked outside to check on things.

I'm thirty-six. Almost dead. Not even born yet. I travel once more through the canal of work this week. I suppose I shouldn't complain. I don't even have to speak to coworkers.

But every hell is different. Every heaven, too.

I stand on deck, surveying the swells of lava. Wave after wave of orange lava, rolling on into infinity. I go below periodically to check the condition of the hull.

I take out my sighting mechanism. As usual, nothing. Oh wait. What's this? Hmm. I do believe I detect the faint trail of a steamer.

"Give chase!"

6

Tuesday.

An afternoon at the Dig. At the site. I fasten my belt on. My gear. Get suited up for the dragon. (The dragon is me.)

I sit here sipping coffee, ignoring my headache. Sirens wail in the distance. The electricity is out again. I am running on battery power.

I descend a long shaft and touch down. I step over corpses, various thoughts. The light dims slightly. I switch on my headlight, begin to move forward. I pass various fantasies. Presently I realize I am walking down a long hall. Fantasies are on my left. Actual engagements are on my right. The fantasies are naturally more pleasurable, more numerous. There are only eighteen actual engagements, but thousands and thousands of fantasies.

I turn down another corridor. Childhood. Years and years of it. Much joy and pain. Another corridor. Religion. Years and years of it. A psychological vehicle. First rudder. I keep going, turn into another tunnel. Young adulthood. I keep walking. First maturity.

Suddenly, I turn and come upon a dream from last night. I recognize it instantly. It is of a woman I never got to kiss. Or even touch. I still have dreams of her, I realize. She's probably fat by now.

I make my way further down a long slope and turn to my left. Down at the end of it there appears to be a river. I recognize myself floating past in a small window in the distance. I walk slowly down there and take a look. I am about twenty-four. In Austin. My hair is long. I am satisfied and content and happy. I am sitting at a table smoking a cigarette.

I keep going. I pass last year, and then last month, and then last week and yesterday. Presently I come up against a dead end. The tunnels simply run out.

I take my pickax and my shovel off my back and start digging and hacking.

I break through after a few minutes. A small hole appears. I keep punching through. A faint shaft of light touches down in the tunnel. I grunt and keep hacking and digging and shoveling. Light begins to flood the area. Soon I make an opening large enough to crawl through. I get down on my hands and knees and make my way over a mound of rubble to the other side. I stand up inside what appears to be a new chamber. I shield my eyes. It is as I suspected: a Power Source.

Yes. For what do we all seek, finally? What do we seek, we archaeologists? We night tunnelers? We seek new Power Sources, new rooms, new chambers. We investigate any new Power Source, any new room, any new chamber.

Every person has one. Every culture. Every religion. Specific *places*. Specific realizations. Yes. We're fascinated, more than anything else, by *types* of Power Sources. By *types* of navigation.

The key to understanding lies in the digestion of the simple realization that art, religion, and mental conditions are all related. They all come from similar areas in the brain. They are three different names for the same thing. Three different versions of it. Three different manifestations of the same phenomenon. The phenomenon of fuel. The phenomenon of the irrational. The phenomenon of the rudder.

7

Saturday.

I am sitting on the back porch, nice and dry, drinking a cup of hot coffee and watching a storm roll in.

Every once in a while, the wind swirls in, ruffling the bottom of my robe. The chill makes the hair on my legs stand up a bit.

Bianca has hopped up to her usual spot to survey the landscape. She licks herself as she sits in her chair, pausing to lift her head up every once in a while at the occasional odd noise before resuming her grooming.

It begins to rain. Large droplets of water are beginning to plop down onto everything now. The swoosh of the wind envelopes the backyard.

Up above the rooftops is a very large oak tree towering over the others.

I look up at it and then down at the little gray shed in the corner of the yard. The shed is very weathered and old-looking. Very long flowers and weeds grow up along each side of the door.

A few birds fly by on their way home. Various blackbirds and blue jays. Seagulls. A few robins and finches darting by, laboring in the wind.

The rain comes steady for about an hour. Very opulent and lush and dense. A symphony of wetness. I sit there.

Service dismissed.

8

The periodic table. Half-life of memory. Isotope of a dream.

I was out earlier. The vacation season is in full swing here.

"Ooh, this is nice. I wonder how far the lake goes."

I sit on a bench. I'm lost, as usual. All evening, endless throngs of people stroll up and down the boardwalk. Lovers, kids, the middle-aged, the elderly. A parade of humans. I sat for the better part of the day absentmindedly staring at the lake, the mountains, and the procession.

9

I am chipping away, still. I feel around for crevices and new entry points. I stand back and study it. I look up and down and peer into shadows and lines and pock marks. I look at it in all types of light. I chip away suddenly on a whim at a previously unused section of the Dig.

I return occasionally with a new map or a new clue purchased at great price in the market. I stand there looking at the wall with my little piece of paper. We try all sorts of different things over and over. We run our hands over smooth edges. We break out the big hammer and knock away at bits of million year old rock.

Meanwhile, the summer heat continues to pour out. Everything is golden. Sun-drenched. Day after day of warmth and heat. I continue to drink it in.

10

I can't write anymore. I can barely put together words. It's sinful.

What a state of affairs. God, it's glorious. I am stupefied at the perfection.

I think life is ridiculous. But I keep living it. In fact, I love it.

Days come and go. I follow urges, eat. Try to sleep. Everything is useless, pointless, cracked, and broken. Gadgets litter our minds. Our minds are full of pomp and circumstance and neuroses and waste.

It's incredible to think how trapped we are, and how free.

I pour another wine.

Olympians, where are you!

The ice cream truck drives by. Memory of a smile. Childhood melody.

I pass out.
Later on, the war.

11

The summer never ended. I'm still there right now. I died there.

It kept going on and on and on. Days and nights and weeks of years. More days, the weekends, night and day again. The cat in the rafters and the pipe in the cupboard. Music at the Shelburne.

The lake, the bicycle rides. The contemplation. The relaxation. The lightning bugs at night. The dream of the meadow. Green valley of home. Vermont.

The Power Source and the drug of the Vermont character is the architecture of the land. The topography, the spell of the open woods and meadows. The sights and sounds of agriculture, the steeples, the churches, the two-lane roads. Early America. In the mold of the Europeans. The French. The British.

Cold, white winters. Mild, green summers. Bright red autumns. Muddy, wet springs.

Over time, you fall under the spell. That, or you escape finally, one of the two.

12

Ah, great life! Many breasted thing! Will I ever get enough?

My chest hurts as usual from smoking marijuana. The Hope of Nothing is the Arrow of Success. A thousand nights of heaven.

The cat keeps interrupting my reveries. Always whining to go inside and out. Silly pussy. Ah, but I understand her plight as well.

I retire to the living room. Pull up a chair to contemplate my latest failure.

10:32 p.m. Disengage.

I'm free-floating now. Eons yawn politely. Lat and Long of courage.

13

I've been outside taking a two-hour sun bath. It's about 75 degrees.

How the days pass. They keep rushing around the bend. Off to strange places. Places one can't look. Victory of forever. Timeline of a triumph. The Spiral heading round again to burst through with ever greater marvels, and more yet to come.

Consider it. Life isn't hell. Life is heaven *and* hell. There is no destination except continued exploration. There is nothing except the synergy and the dimensions of this universe. This universe is the end-all and be-all of everything. It is capable of anything you can dream up, and more still. It has always been here. It will always be here. It spews realities, dreams, little things called men.

Humans are capable of masterworks. Masterworks of reality. Experiments lasting centuries, millennia, eons. The human brain is the fruit. It is ripe. It is capable of any political or cultural reality imaginable. It is the race of animals! It is the race of gods! For we are the animals! For we are the gods!

14

The jets keep flying overhead. They've been doing maneuvers. They fly directly over downtown Burlington almost every day now. The noise from the afterburners rattles the windows. Little squadrons of four and six planes each, all their movements synchronized. Occasionally one will bank off and the others appear to give chase.

Yesterday the noise was overwhelming. I couldn't work. Finally I went into the backyard and pulled up a chair and just watched them. They would fly out west and bank, turn, and head right back over the backyard at maybe one thousand feet in the air. At a certain point right after they had turned, they would fire their afterburners for a few seconds and come screaming directly over the house. I was sitting there looking up at them with my hands over my ears.

(Bianca! We're under attack! Run!)

They did this over and over and over, for about an hour. Each time they came in you could get a solid look at the plane's underbellies as the formation raced by.

It got old eventually.

15

Next day.

Here they come again. The jets. Christ.
Fifteen minutes later, I'm laying on the couch.

I'm lazy. I laugh at most everything. I am fascinated by rain. Death. The spiders in the basement. I think I need to make some more coffee. Or perhaps some tea instead.
Tap tap tap. It's occupied!
I fold my hands. I sit in my chair. Silent. Content. Mesmerized. Breathing is a miracle. Ah, the jets again. Jesus Christ.
Here they come. The windows are rattling now. Ridiculous! I demand silence! Where must I go for silence? Where, oh tell me where?

One just streaked by at maximum volume. It wasn't so much a plane coming by as a large, thirty-million-dollar bullet whistling a few hundred feet overhead.

They're doing it over and over now. Surely this has to be a demonstration or part of an air show of some sort. This can't be normal procedure.
All the same, I keep waiting for one to crash into the house, or accidentally fire a missile, or something.

I go outside. The neighbors are all standing around in their front yards, everyone milling about and chattering.

A little excitement, a little noise has awakened them from their slumber. Everyone outside wondering and babbling and squawking and ooh-ing and ah-ing.

"Well, Charley works up at the base and he was saying . . ."

"My cousin says they've been doing . . ."

Several more jets curve around in a giant arc to the north and then turn sharply west and switch on the afterburners. They shriek by directly overhead. Everyone holds their ears.

And then it all dies down as suddenly as it began. They all fly off. After a few minutes, everything is quiet again.

I walk back inside and sit around, waiting to see if there's going to be another round of action.

16

Evening prayers.

The sun has set like a dandelion. The sun is my heart, broken. A memory-strewn daydream, footsteps making their way to hell.

I have no idea what anything means.

My days beg coins in the open market. My nights bathe virgins in gold bathtubs.

My days hike mountains for mercy. My nights sculpt ruby eyes.

I wash clothes in muddy rivers, swim laps in blue champagne.

Sweet God, oh angel of my death.

Life is the friend of a thousand worlds. I ache for it as no man ever has.

17

Twenty minutes of eternity. A thimbleful of nirvana. Tea for all the children. Crumpets for the saints.

The nights keep coming. The days. The afternoons. I dream of soft thighs. Garters. Creamy stockings.

The world stews in its own juices. Murder. Madness. The usual emotions.

We mean less than the air.

I sit here clearing my throat.

I keep sneezing. The pills I took don't seem to be working. I go in the bathroom and rip another one out of the package. I cast a perfunctory glance at the warnings on the label again. "Do not exceed recommended dosage. May cause marked drowsiness." Good. That's what I like. Marked drowsiness.

I dream of opiates, fair bosoms, Caligula's boats. Italy. Diana's Mirror.

I take the pill. Drink some water.

I sit and stare off for ten minutes. I walk back to the couch.

Lights! Camera! Cough!

I open up a beer. Debate heating up a little something to eat.

"Titus! Assemble the legions! There's food in the kitchen. Pastries, peanuts, pork. And the sweet Egyptian beer that tastes like Chardonnay."

"Maximus! Lend me your ear. Your orchard. Your daughter."

"Gilletticus! Avedicus! Noxzemus! Pray, anoint my feet with all the latest gels and lotions."

I put down the pipe again.

"Let us retire to Diana's Mirror for games and fornication."

I sit back down on the couch. The Holy Spirit has left me. I'm feeling drowsy already. I should have read the directions. Wait, I *did* read the directions.

I stretch out. I giggle. All right. Enough. *Auf Wiedersehen.*

18

Everything is pissy. Agitated. There's always tension. Down to the last, restless, bitchy little atom. We are trapped between knowing and not knowing. Between wanting and not knowing.

We eat. Watch movies. Copulate. We fear boredom as much as hunger. More than danger, even.

A few thousand years pass. People keep dying, living. Living, dying. Civilizations emerge, recede into the distance. We have mental pods. Pharmaceuticals. Custom realities. World War IX. Companies replace countries, complete with their own constitutions, cultures, armies, etc. They trade with other companies. The problem is antibiotic production.

A hundred thousand years pass. Influenza has decimated the population. A dog barks somewhere. The weather is warm. Packs of wild dogs roam the hinterlands, as well as constricting snakes in the southeastern United States. The snakes and the dogs are top predators. The dogs get very large. The Florida Everglades stretch out over several states.

A million years pass. Northern Canada is the population center of the planet. There are approximately ninety thousand people left. They live inside a dome. They are all tour guides.

19

You don't even have to move. Everything moves for you.

People think Rome is in the past. Rome is in the future also.

Another storm is rolling through. The wind is blowing. I couldn't be happier. Storms never fail to excite me. I feel invigorated, truly alive in stormy weather.

I've come to the conclusion that I am borderline autistic. No matter! Heave ho, you ninnies! You fine china!

The day yawns. I yawn. We all yawn. The entire world should fall asleep for several decades. What are we all but bad sleep and overworked brains? We need to get off the amphetamines. Or maybe we need to increase the dosage, one of the two.

I can't decide which is better: not enough or too much.

I stir my soup. My mind.

I'm sick with allergies and hopped up on cold medication, vodka and orange juice, marijuana, ibuprofen, insomnia, etc. I'm hammered. Off in another time zone.

It's Labor Day weekend. I laugh. Decide to go run a tub full of hot water for a bath.

I can't stop sneezing now. The human body and its various afflictions and abnormalities. It's vaguely humorous. I'm so altered, I can't really get upset at it. It's rather fascinating to become disassociated with your body.

I want to live to be ten thousand. Yes! I must see what keeps happening!

For example, at the end of the "companies rule the planet" stage? What replaces that when it begins to break down? Things will have come full circle. Back to the tribal stage.

By then, we will be out in outer space more than likely, prepping that for treatment as well.

20

I sit here staring off at the floor. The light is on in the kitchen and I am looking in there at the floor and the design of the tile. The living room is pleasantly dark.

I'm still sick. I can't stop sneezing. Everything I do is an endless repetition of nonsense. Trips to the bathroom for toilet paper. Various absurdities.

I go to the store for a purchase. I buy wine, carrots, orange juice, smoked turkey, and cold medicine.

Life is a merry-go-round of death. Each day, a trip through chance and old age. Youth and women. Burnout and cancer. With toy lungs. Leverage. Lack of options.

We're all addicted to ass. To intoxicants. To ourselves. It's like a machine set to "never."

21

October. Atoms. Funny math.

The sun has set. I'm sitting here watching the day slip away. The light is fading. I'm looking outside and I ache. I'm hungry.

Ah, the light and the leaves on the trees silhouetted against the clouds. The paintbrush and the palette of it all. The green firs. The contrast. The memories bubbling up.

Autumn is the bringer of memories. Autumn is the god of memory. Faded pictures. Little moods. Little days. Fleeting images from long ago.

I look over at the fire, and then out the window again, at the leaves swirling across the sidewalk. Little dervishes of color. Little reds and golds.

I'm weak from not eating. My hands are shaking. But I'd rather sit here and not disturb myself.

This is the totality, the summation of all possibility. There is no garden more fruitful, no breast more delightful. The fuel . . . ah, the fuel is all you need. Ah, the beginning. The end. The fuel is all you need.

22

It's been getting dark for about a thousand years.

I yawn. Atoms make love. Molecules reunite with old friends.

It's Sunday night. It's hell. It's about eleven.

I'm standing in the kitchen drinking root beer.

The stink of reality and the fresh air of reality. Agonies of hours.

Timeline: Vermont. Date: irrelevant. The cat sits grooming herself. The sun still warms the land.

Seasons flicker out in the street. Mountain ranges fall away. Silicon birds. Butterflies of our urges.

I sit looking out the window at little spots of brightly colored green and yellow.

A car drives by. It gets dark.

I sit here breathing.

The Dig awaits. The jackhammer and the tools and the pickax of our love. Ah, the intent. The need for the vein. The lust for the vein.

The Spiral laughs again.

23

Vermont was made for me, and I for it. Too bad I probably have to leave it someday.

I disembarked this afternoon on my eighty-seventh bicycle ride.

I ride down to the end of Gazo Avenue and Ethan Allen Parkway and head north across Route 127 and onto the bike path where it runs parallel to the road for a ways down to Ethan Allen's place.

After a few minutes you coast to the entrance of the woods and to the paths that take you out to the Public Farms and to the Ethan Allen Homestead. I've done it so, so many times.

I turn in down the little hill and through a gate and immediately am in the soft, little thicket that tunnels down beside the empty field on the left. There is a steep embankment on the right that leads up to the homestead. The effect is that of a little burrow through the undergrowth. The path is fairly separated from the field, and for some reason, this spot has always struck me as the perfect place to set up booby traps to defend a military assault on the homestead just up the hill. It makes me think of World War I, European battlefields, various artillery vehicles hidden behind the brush waiting to unleash.

I keep pedaling and begin to veer right a bit and soon the field falls away on the left and is replaced by a shady, mowed, clearing with a landing where you can launch a canoe onto the Winooski River.

I enter the forest proper, and the trail continues on in a giant arc through the woods to the right for a ways. A little finger of the river snakes around beside the path on the left and it is here that the trail is darkest after night has fallen. (Usually I have to stop here and pedal very slowly and carefully when I am riding at night.)

Presently, I exit the forest and veer back to the left and come upon the second parting through the undergrowth that goes on for another 150 meters or so. Then I turn back into the woods one more time and come upon a small bridge overlooking the dank, insect-infested, backwater tributary of the creek. Once over the bridge, you go up a hill where you are greeted by another long path through a tunnel of grass.

Eventually I come out beside the Winooski River curving around again and on the right is the large field with the geese and the ducks and the deer. Then you wander along through various public and private farms, making various turns here and there and generally just following the path out to whichever farm or road strikes your fancy.

I loiter for a while. Turn around. Again. And again and again.

24

I sit at night in the Nothing. I worship the Nothing. The Fountain.

I sit here stirring my tea. Amazed. Bewildered. A monkey. I hear crickets outside.

The screen door creaks. I sit here. Curious. Intoxicated. A hairless little ape. Bipedal locomotion. A little hominid.

Being alive is like standing in the front of a long line at a certain point on the side of a mountain path that is circling around and up and then looking slowly back down the path at the long procession of people all marching and coming to a halt behind you and stretching all the way down the mountain and out into the meadow as far as the eye can see. Being alive is then realizing simultaneously that the line will soon continue on past you for eons and eternities to come and that the wave of consciousness and awareness that you are now riding will soon give way beneath you and roll past you and drop you back down behind it and that History will keep rolling on away from you into the horizon until it becomes a tiny little speck and disappears.

In the end, it means less than an atom. The universe itself doesn't even know what makes it tick. It speaks in different languages. We are one of its languages. It speaks through us. In turn, we try to recreate it in our image but it doesn't work this way.

There is no escaping it: We were made to soak the earth in our blood. A few decades of peace and prosperity are the biggest miracle in life. A few centuries would be too much to ask for.

25

I sit scribbling formulas. Dangling chance. I sit at night working it out with a pencil. The hypotenuse of life never adds up to a right angle. Forty-five degrees of never. Cosine of maybe. Solve for xxx.

26

Saturday.

The minotaur of my love waits patiently in the dream.

On a whim, I decide to rent a motorboat and go for a ride on Lake Champlain.

I park the car and walk down to the docks. There is a tiny building with a Dutch door. The top half is open. There is a bearded youth inside running the place. I tell him I would like to rent the large motorboat for four hours. He nods and produces a contract. I pay him. We talk about the contract. I sign various waivers and disclaimers informing me that if I get killed it's not their fault. I put my initials on everything, give it back, and we head down to the water. He keeps asking me if I have ever been out in a boat before.

The vessel is a little sixteen-foot Boston Whaler with a 75-horsepower Mercury outboard engine. The console is on the right side, with passenger seats to the left and rear, and a small lounging area up in the front. The boat is white and silver. We get in. He goes over various instructions. The engine and the prop are my responsibility, and the prop has to come back all in one piece, with no cuts or marks or visual damage of any kind whatsoever.

"Yes, yes," I tell him. "Don't worry about a thing. I've logged millions of hours."

He tells me the tank is half full, but if I anticipate doing a lot of running we can fill it up.

I politely ask that we fill it up.

He turns the key. The starter whines and turns over, and in a second or two, the engine comes to life. A few rings of blue smoke come out of the exhaust.

I stand there looking around. Boats of all kinds are crowded in next to one another. People are milling about. The sun is out.

He lets the motor idle for a few minutes and then unties the rope and throws it in and we ease away from the dock and slowly make our way down to the fueling station. He pulls up, cuts off the engine, and gets out to fill the tank while I hold the boat steady. A few more last-minute instructions and then he cranks it up again and hands it over to me and pushes me off.

I squeeze the throttle and gently put the engine in gear. I wave. He waves back and wishes me a good trip.

I go slowly through the "no wake zone" and make my way out to the open lake. The sun is lovely. The seagulls scream overhead.

I have a smirk on my face. I turn around and look at the motor.

I'm standing up with one hand on the wheel, one hand on the throttle, the boat bubbling and humming along. I pass a yacht. Further down, the *Spirit of Ethan Allen* has just come back from an outing and is preparing to moor down the dock a bit. I look back to the front, pass the "no wake" marker now.

I look back at the engine again and then at the open lake ahead. I push the throttle forward smoothly, and the boat surges ahead. I floor it, and soon the boat is up on a plane and whisking across the water at a heady clip. I giggle. My hair is blowing. I turn around to look at the wake and then up at the various gauges on the control panel. Speed: 32 miles per hour. RPMs: 3,800. Gas: full. Engine Temperature: normal. Oil pressure: normal.

I look back up. A few minutes pass. I am now passing over a spot where American warships rest in peace at the bottom of the lake after a nasty engagement with the British at the Battle of Valcour Island in 1776. I smile. God bless their souls.

I decide to head north.

The lake stretches out another sixty miles in front of me, all the way to Canada. It also extends south for another sixty miles or so. It's about ten miles wide.

The engine whines in my ears. I throttle back just a bit to cruising speed. The lake is calm. The water looks like glass. Miles and miles of it.

I look up. The Adirondacks of New York are on the left, and the Green Mountains of Vermont are on the right. The sunlight plays on the water. The sky yawns overhead.

Gradually the sound of the engine begins to decrease.

I think vaguely of old friends. Old loves. New life. New epochs. New civilizations.

Suddenly, a large flock of geese on my right takes flight at the approach of the boat. I smile and angle the boat over into them. They start flapping mightily. Out over the water, they have nowhere to go except higher up. For a little while, they are only about three or four feet off the water and can only fly about the same speed as the boat. I maneuver the boat slowly in among them, looking alternately at them and then up ahead, and back and forth. I start snickering. I throttle back and let them get in front of me again, and then I switch to the other side and drift up again. I turn slowly into them from the opposite angle. They attempt to bank off, and I keep heading in. They cut back once more right over the boat. One is flapping its wings almost directly over the bow now. They're all around the boat, almost within arm's reach. They're all squawking, and I am snickering and giggling.

Finally they begin to gain altitude, creeping slowly upward. I keep laughing. I stay beside them for a little while. They keep banking off and get higher and higher and higher.

I look up. The lake keeps whizzing by.
I trim the motor up a bit.

The engine hums.

Terry Midkiff was born in Houston in 1970. He grew up in North Carolina and Texas. His work has appeared in *Mobius, The Poetry Magazine.*